HAUNTING AT ELMWOODS MANSION

By: Katherine Buchwald

Order this book online at www.trafford.com
or email orders@trafford.com

Most Trafford titles are also available at major online book retailers.

Printed in Victoria, BC, Canada.

ISBN: 978-1-4120-2546-1 (sc)
ISBN: 978-1-4122-2291-4 (e)

Our mission is to efficiently provide the world's finest, most comprehensive book publishing service, enabling every author to experience success. To find out how to publish your book, your way, and have it available worldwide, visit us online at www.trafford.com

 www.trafford.com

North America & international
toll-free: 1 888 232 4444 (USA & Canada)
phone: 250 383 6864 ♦ fax: 812 355 4082

Dedicated to my parents

Thank you for always being there and taking away my

childhood fears.

CHAPTER ONE

It was a cool and sunny Friday morning in mid-June as the minivan moved down the road away from the house in Benton Hills. Slowly the house disappeared from sight as Melody turned forward in her seat and buckled her seat belt firmly in place. The sun beamed brightly on her face as they made their way to the interstate. As they drove along, Melody listened to her parents talking about her father's new job in New Hampshire. Her father had dreamed for years about starting his own company. Now it was about to come

3

true. For twelve years he had worked for an architectural firm that was only a few miles from the house in Benton Hills, Pennsylvania. Now he was about to take on his own firm and it made him a little nervous. It would take a few months, but he was convinced that everything would work out well once he got started. Melody's mom, JoAnne, continually coached him, telling him that he was a natural at running things and that his own firm would not be any different.

Even though the thought of his own business and a new house was exciting, dad was worried. He knew that Melody and Belinda had grown up in the house in Benton Hills. Danville, New Hampshire would be far away from the life they knew. This would be a big change for the girls and he hoped that they would not have any problems fitting into a new life style. They would be making new friends and attending a new school, and he was concerned about the impact that it would have on them. Still, he was anxious to get back to work and settle into their new home.

Melody leaned forward in her seat and picked up the

neatly folded map that had slid partially under her dad's driver seat. She opened the map and began to track the distance. Following the lines, she stretched her fingers apart about one inch for each ten miles. She knew that they had already been traveling for quite a few hours. It would only be about another hour or so before they would finally reach their destination. Melody sighed with relief as she looked over at her sister Belinda, who was sound asleep. Watching her sleep made Melody feel tired, but she was too excited to sleep. The four were up very early that morning and Melody felt weary, but she couldn't miss anything along the way to the new house. Too many things were bothering her and she wondered how soon she would make new friends.

She also thought about the night before, when they had gone over to their grandparents' house to say good-bye. Melody's parents had promised them that they would visit often, but Melody did not feel satisfied with that. Grandma was so upset about the move, and she worried about her. Grandma loved being near her family and her visits with her grandchildren every weekend made her extremely happy. Melody could always see her grand parents whenever she wanted, and it was all about to change.

Mom and Grandma would make a big meal for everyone every Sunday. During the summer months, Melody and Belinda would go out to pick fresh corn from the field. They also picked fresh strawberries to go with the homemade shortcakes Grandma always made. In the winter they sat by the big picture window in the living room and watched it snow. Grandma Drake would sometimes bring out the old family photo album, giving them the history of past generations.

Papa loved to take the girls out to the barn to visit the horses. Almost half of the thirty- acre farm was wooded and they would sometimes go out on a trail ride that lasted for hours. Melody would miss all of those wonderful things and wondered how often they would get to see the horses. She felt as though she would not be able to bare all the new changes that were about to happen. Her life was about to be ripped apart, and there was nothing that she could do about it.

Melody would also miss Scamper, Molly's filly that she had given birth to only four months ago. Molly was a beautiful Appaloosa quarter horse that Belinda prized most and absolutely adored. She had a dark coloring with bright white spots that covered her rump. She thought about the day that Scamper was born and how gentle Molly was with him, pampering her baby until he stood on all four legs.

Papa owned four horses, but out of all of them, Melody loved Cricket the most. He was a beautiful American Saddle bred who had the most graceful gate she had ever seen. Every time she would enter the barn, Cricket would peak his head out of the stall looking for carrots and the sugar cubes she had hidden in her pockets. Melody would pull out one of the sugar cubes or a tasty piece of carrot and place it on her flattened palm. Cricket would gently take the food from her hand and then with his ears pointed forward and alert, he would stare at her with his brown shiny eyes. Melody would talk to him and he seemed to listen closely to her every word as she ran her fingers through his long black mane. She would turn and lean her back on his stall door. Cricket would rest his head on her shoulder as she talked to him, and she knew that he was her best friend. Melody thought about how much she would miss him and how he would be lost without all of those wonderful sugar cubes and carrots.

About two months ago, their parents left Melody and Belinda with their grandparents and flew to New Hampshire to see the new house and sign papers. The girls couldn't come along because school was still in session. Mom told them about what the new house looked like and how much she thought the girls would love the new place. Mom was excited as well and had already started planning where she would place each piece of furniture. Decorating, planning, and organizing were first and foremost on mom's mind; but Melody couldn't see the excitement in that. How could someone be excited about cleaning, organizing, and decorating, it just seemed like a lot of work. Melody had other things on her mind.

Mr. Drake had always pushed his daughters to succeed and work through life with an open mind. Melody was always a very inquisitive and highly motivated young girl. She saw excitement when she thought about the places she could go and the friends she could make. What would the new school be like? That was something Melody had not thought of before. They never moved before, or ever had to think about a new school. Her parents visited the new school during the time they spent in New Hampshire looking at the new house, and thought the girls would enjoy it a lot.

Mom and dad told the girls about Danville Middle School before they left for their trip. Thinking back to that, Melody could feel a lump grow in her throat. The fear of having to make new friends was really starting to set in. It is a 7th and 8th grade school; therefore, Belinda would be in the same school with her since she was only a year younger. At least Melody wouldn't feel alone. It was only the third week of June and Melody and Belinda would have all summer to prepare. But now she would have to start all over again and make new friends.

Belinda shifted back and forth in her seat and started to open her eyes. "Where are we?" she said, rubbing her eyes. Melody leaned over and pointed to the spot on the map she was still clutching in her hands. "It is not too far now, I figure that we are less than an hour from the house," Melody responded.

Belinda extended her arms above her head, her fingertips touching the ceiling of the minivan, stretched, and then settled calmly in her seat. She was dazed from her long nap, and didn't seem coherent enough to realize what Melody had just told her. For the next few minutes Belinda just sat there staring out the window watching the mile markers pass by. The drive from Pennsylvania was longer than she had anticipated, and she was just as anxious as Melody to get to the new house.

For the next few minutes the girls listened to their parents talking in soft voices. Then their mother turned around in her seat and looked back at them. "We were thinking about stopping for dinner before we get to the house, are you two hungry?" she asked.

Both girls looked up at their mother and agreed. It had been several hours since their last stop. Everyone was feeling a little stiff and felt the need to get up and walk around. Besides, Belinda always seemed to be hungry, all of their stomachs were yelling at them.

Dad proceeded to guide the van off the freeway and down the off ramp and stopped at the red light. Through Belinda's sliding door window, the girls could see a large blue sign. It had pictures of a knife and fork, a gas pump, and an advertisement for a Sleepy Time Inn; one mile, with an arrow that pointed north. With that, the light turned green and dad made a left turn heading north on Silver Creek Road. Melody slouched down into her seat and sighed. It was almost 5 o'clock as she glanced down at her watch. Adding in time for dinner, it would be close to 7 o'clock before they would arrive at the new house.

Just as the big blue sign had predicted, about a mile

down the road was a place called "Mary Ann's Diner." The place looked old, but well kept. Dad turned the van into the parking lot and found a space close to the main entrance of the diner. Four large semi-trucks were parked at the far end of the parking lot. Belinda opened the sliding door next to her seat and stepped out of the van. Melody followed slightly crouched as she made her way out. The girls stretched for a moment and then followed their parents into the diner. "The place was clean and pleasant for being a truck stop," Melody thought.

A waitress with a pleasant smile walked over to them as they entered the restaurant. She wore a white dress, and a red and white checked apron. "Four?" she said as she pick up the menus that were nestled in a wooden slot next to her. "This way please," she said, as she quickly seated them in a booth by the window and handed them their menus. She checked the sugar and cream container's and then turned and left. Soon the waitress was back and set a glass of ice water next to each of them. "Can I take your orders?" she asked.

Dad looked over at the girls and they each began to place their orders. While they waited for dinner to be served, Belinda and Melody talked about what they were going to do once they reached the new house. They knew it would be a long and busy night and the girls were getting anxious. Their thoughts began to sound much like their mother's, thinking about where they wanted their furniture, and how big their rooms were. There were a lot of questions and the girls were beginning to feel a little more nervous about the move than excited.

About twenty minutes had passed as mom looked away from the window, where she had been staring, seeming to be in deep thought. "That must be for us", mom said looking over at the waitress who was making her way to their table with a large platter. After setting out all of the dinners the waitress looked at the girls and then over at Mr. and Mrs. Drake. "Enjoy your meals," she said smiling.

Throughout dinner the girls talked with their parents about the new house. There wasn't too much in the van that they would have to unpack for their first night. The only large item they would have to move that night would be the television which dad could not live without in the evenings. The rest of it was just suitcases and a box that mom had packed with food for that night and early the following morning. The big job would start when the moving truck arrived the next morning. As they continued talking, the waitress walked over after serving the table next to them.

"Are you on vacation? I have never seen you in here before. It is really quite a beautiful town," the waitress said, "Usually we only see regulars around here."

Mom looked up at the waitress in amazement. "Actually we just purchased a house in Danville a few months back, and are now just moving in." she replied.

"That is over where the old Marshall mansion is. It is the only house on Elm Drive and it sits far back in the woods. Everyone says that place is haunted and creepy," the waitress said. "Everyone steers clear of that old place if you know what I mean." The waitress took a long look at Belinda and

14

Melody and then replied, "Enjoy your meals." Then she hurried off.

"I wonder why she seemed so nervous, it was almost like we said something terrible," Mom said as she started eating her meal. Melody looked at her sister with a look of adventure on her face. "A haunted house," she thought, "what could be more intriguing than that?"

Soon after dinner was over, dad left a tip on the table and went up to pay the bill. Then they headed out to the van and started back on their way. Most of the way all the girls could see was fields and every so often an old house and a few farms. Belinda was still munching on some french fries that she had left from dinner. Melody grabbed the map and began to figure out their location. There was only about twenty-five minutes of traveling to go, but it seemed like an eternity. Impatiently waiting to get to the new house, Melody decided to look up Elm Drive. The map indicated that the old haunted house was only a few blocks away from their new house!

CHAPTER TWO

After about fifteen minutes, they passed a sign that read "Danville, population 8734". "So much for seven o'clock," Melody thought. It was now almost quarter to eight. Belinda had settled back and closed her eyes again after they left the restaurant. Melody wasn't sure if she had fallen asleep, so she didn't mention anything. She thought about the population count, and how small the town was. Benton Hill's, Pennsylvania was nearly three times larger than Danville. Most likely the school is small, and most likely she would be bored, having a hard time making friends. Not a thought that she wished to have again. Maybe things would not be as bad as she thought. She kept glancing down at her watch. Soon the van slowed and they turned and started up the driveway. Melody shook Belinda's shoulder, "Hey, we're here, wake up!" Belinda opened her eyes and looked around. It was just starting to get dark outside.

There was a garage behind house that was illuminated from the headlights of the van. The house was dark and the girls could only get a partial view of what it looked like. Dad parked the van in front of the house. Mom got out of the van and started to walk up to the house. Melody and Belinda opened the sliding door and got out. They walked to the back of the van with their father and began collecting some of their things before they headed toward the house.

Although it was just starting to get dark, the girls could see the large two-story house. It was painted a soft yellow and had large white shutters on each side of all of the windows. There were two large windows, one on each side of the front door and four tall narrow windows that lined the second story in the front of the house. A small curved sidewalk led from the driveway to the front porch and was lined on one side with newly planted spring flowers. A large tree stood in the middle of the front yard and seemed to shelter the sidewalk with its branches. It seemed to be a quaint and well-kept house. Morning would certainly reveal more of what the house looked like.

Mom walked up onto the front porch that extended the full length of the front of the house. She unlocked the front door and stepped inside, leaving it wide open. Soon she found the light switch and flipped on the porch lights. The house looked huge, the girls thought, as they made their way up the sidewalk. It was definitely bigger than their house in Pennsylvania. A decorative spindled railing surrounded the entire porch and down the front steps adding a welcoming feeling to the old house. The old wood steps creaked as the girls walked up on to the porch.

A large staircase that led to the upstairs greeted them warmly as they entered through the front door. Melody and Belinda placed their rolled up sleeping bags and over-night cases on the floor of the large foyer and walked up the steps to the second floor. Both of the girls looked around at the three bedrooms they had to choose from. After only a few minutes they both had figured out which rooms they wanted. The third room was left for dad who had claimed the last room for his study. The only other room that was left was the master bedroom, which was on the opposite end of the second floor. The rooms were large with hardwood floors and big tall windows. Melody's room had a window seat, but Belinda felt that her room was better because it was larger and had a walk-in closet.

Melody remembered her father telling her and her sister that the house was over 100 years old! As Melody and Belinda investigated the house further, they found that all of the rooms were very large. The entire house carried the scent of fresh paint. They knew right away that they would have a lot of space for their things and they realized that their Mom was correct; they would really enjoy living here.

The moving van that carried all of their furniture would be arriving early the next morning and the girls were deciding where they wanted everything to go. When they were both satisfied with where they were going to sleep, the two went back downstairs to the foyer and collected their over-night cases and sleeping bags to take back up to their rooms. Once back in their rooms they began to settle in.

The limbs of the large tree outside Melody's window swayed in the soft breeze. They made a swooshing sound as the limbs lightly brushed up against the house. Melody thought about the noise, and wondered if she would be able to sleep. Then she walked over and picked up her sleeping bag and unrolled it on the floor, and went to talk with Belinda who was in her room.

"I feel like I am not going to get any sleep tonight, but I feel exhausted," Melody told Belinda "And I just can't get that waitress off my mind either. She was so sure about that house being haunted. We've never seen a real haunted house before."

"She was kind of strange," Belinda replied, "The Marshall mansion must be a big story around here, but I am sure you will get to sleep... I know I will."

Melody knew that her sister could sleep even if the house was falling down around her. However, Melody was feeling restless and out of touch with things. It would take a while to get used to all of the changes. She also thought about the Marshall mansion... her intuitive side was getting the best of her. Melody and Belinda talked about it for a while, wondering why it seemed that the waitress was trying to keep them from going to the old mansion. Checking out a haunted house could prove to be a lot of fun and maybe one day they would do just that.

The girls could hear their parents moving around downstairs. They were moving the few things they had brought with them into the house from the van. Melody followed Belinda down the stairs to see if there was something they could help with. Melody walked through the dining room and into the kitchen where she found her mother standing in front of the open cabinets, her hand rubbing her chin in deep thought. "Did you need any help?" Melody asked.

Her mother, a bit startled, turned and looked at Melody. "No, there's not too much to do for now. I think we have it all under control, but thanks," she said, seeming far away. With that, Melody turned and headed out of the kitchen. She took two steps and was stopped by a loud scream from her mother. Melody turned back around and looked, her mother was now standing in the middle of the kitchen jumping from one foot to the other, her hands halfway into the air and her face had turned pale. "Did you see that?"

her mother said with a shaken voice. Melody looked around the kitchen, "see what?" she replied.

Her mother took a step back and looked around the floor. "That!" she screamed, as a mouse ran across the floor and behind one of the boxes they had just brought in from the van. Melody jumped back a step into the dining room and looked slowly around the kitchen. Mom grabbed a broom that stood in the corner of the kitchen. She began to shuffle it back and forth behind the mouse, trying to guide it away from the boxes. Soon it shot out and ran to the middle of the room. Mom shuffled the broom behind it and guided the little mouse to the back door and outside. "I just hate those things," her mother said, feeling a bit more at ease as she closed the back door. "I hope we don't see any more of those nasty little creatures again."

"Me too, but are you okay now?" Melody asked. Her mother reassured her that she was okay. Melody turned the corner from the kitchen, through the dining room and into the foyer, before heading outside to the van. Belinda and her father were just getting the last few things out and shutting the hatch. Melody grabbed a few things that were cradled in her sister's arms and turned and looked back at the house. "How long do you think it will take to get used to all of this?" Melody asked her father.

"Maybe it will be a couple of months, or only a few weeks. Don't worry, everything will work out okay," he said. David hoped that his family would adjust sooner than later… everything would just take time.

By this time mom had turned on the living room and dining room lights. The light beamed through the front windows of the house and gave more light to the front porch. This is home, Melody thought and began to walk up to the house.

Everyone was exhausted after the long drive. Dad had already set up the television in one corner on the living room floor, something he never could live without in the evenings. Mom and dad were propped up on a few pillows that were tossed on the floor when the girls came in to join them. For a

couple of hours they enjoyed a movie and popcorn that mom
made for them before they went upstairs for the night.

Belinda was out fast even though she had slept in the
van on the way to Danville, but Melody laid her head back on
her folded pillow and stared at the ceiling. She started to
think about her friends back in Pennsylvania and how much
she missed them and her nice warm bed. She wondered if she
would ever really feel comfortable in the new house. Melody
decided to pull her mp3 player from her backpack. She
placed her headphones firmly to her ears and tried to relax.
Maybe the music would ease her mind. 'Tomorrow could not
come soon enough,' she thought, as she drifted slowly to
sleep.

The entire night Melody was restless. She would
sleep for a short time and then wake again. She kept
dreaming of people she had never seen before. At one point,
after waking up about six times, Melody almost gave up the
idea of sleeping. Finally around 4:00 a.m., she fell into a
deep sleep.

CHAPTER THREE

It was 6:45 a.m. and JoAnne decided it was time to get the girls up from their slumber. It would give them just over an hour to get dressed and have breakfast before the moving van would arrive. She got up from the porch swing and walked into the house. From the bottom of the steps she yelled up to the girls, "Come on you two, rise and shine, time to get up and get going!" she said. Shortly after she could hear Melody and Belinda each yell back, acknowledging that

26

they were awake. Then mom went back out to the porch where she was having coffee with dad.

Belinda was up and into the bathroom before Melody completely opened her eyes. Melody took a nice long stretch, she could feel her exhaustion from deep inside and her brain didn't want to work. She was lost without the alarm clock that used to sit on her bedside table. She felt grateful that most everything would be back to normal by the end of the day. She couldn't handle the idea of going one more minute without her closet full of clothes.

Thankfully, she had not forgotten to pack an backpack with her make-up, hair dryer and one set of clean clothes… the morning would have been a disaster otherwise. As soon as Melody heard Belinda open the bathroom door and walk down the hall passed her room, she unzipped her sleeping bag, grabbed her things and went stumbling out of the room to get ready to start the day.

Dad had gone into town and picked up breakfast and everyone was sitting out on the front porch when Melody came downstairs. "What time is it?" Melody asked. Belinda, who was sitting on the porch railing sipping on orange juice looked up at Melody and replied, "It's 7:30. I heard you mumbling last night; maybe you were talking in your sleep." Melody, feeling like only half of her had made it downstairs, dizzily looked at Belinda and nodded. Everyone quickly ate breakfast and mom cleaned up.

The moving truck would arrive around 8 o'clock with two men to move everything into the house. Dad called the moving company at 7 o'clock and was reassured that everything was moving on schedule.

It was now just a few minutes past eight, and the moving van was backing into the driveway. They backed the truck all the way up to the porch and rested a ramp between the porch and the truck. Then one of the men went up to dad, who was standing in the front yard, and had him sign a piece of paper before they started unloading.

First, the movers brought the furniture off the truck. Mom guided the men as they came in with the furniture, and

showed them where to place each piece. Then it was the
boxes that were each labeled with the names of the rooms on
them... kitchen, master bedroom and so forth. They were
each placed in their designated rooms around the house.
Within about four hours, the movers had completed
unloading. Mom wrote out a check for them and sent them
on their way.

Everyone pitched in helping to move furniture around
and empty boxes. The girls helped their mother for a while in
the kitchen, unwrapping dishes and putting away glasses and
silverware. By lunch time the kitchen was basically
organized. Even though mom knew that she would end up re-
organizing a second time, she was thrilled and decided on
what they would make that evening for dinner.

Dad had been upstairs all morning putting up curtain
rods and setting up his new study. He was anxious to get
started right away with his new company and everything had
to be in its proper place. Mom brought a few potted plants

29

upstairs to his office to brighten it up a little before starting lunch.

After lunch the girls took off for their rooms and began to push furniture into place and unpack more boxes. Melody began to organize all of her things in the dressers and closet and then went into the hall where the mattresses were leaning against the wall. Their father helped them put their bed frames together and move the mattresses into place. Soon everything did seem like it was almost back to normal, except for the only things that would always be missing, their grandparents and friends back in Pennsylvania. Melody thought back to the look on grandma's face as they left her house and started toward their new life.

Melody and Belinda had talked the night before about how much they missed their grandparents and wondered how long it would be until they would see them again. It could be weeks or months before that would happen. Melody decided that she would take some time that evening and write a letter to her grandparents and one to each of her friends back in

Pennsylvania. She was sure that it would make her feel better to stay in close contact with everyone that she had left behind. Until then, there was still a lot to do to get organized. There were piles of boxes everywhere to be unpacked. Dad wanted all of the empty boxes folded down and on the tree lawn after dinner.

Melody finished up in her room by putting her teddy bears on the window seat, and then she went downstairs to take a look around and see how mom and dad were doing. Some of the boxes were pushed to the outside of the rooms, but everything looked comfortable, just like mom always liked it. The girls always called her a 'clean freak,' because everything had to be just so.

Seeing that everything was under control on the main floor Melody decided to sit out on the front porch steps, like she did when they went to their grandparent's house back in Pennsylvania. "I have to stop this," Melody thought to herself, "this is home now and Pennsylvania is in the past, unless we visit grandma and papa."

Shortly after Melody went outside, Belinda too had finished and joined her sister on the porch. "Hey you... finished?" Belinda asked.

"Yeah, but I don't feel completely organized, and I almost feel like I lost some things, and I know that I didn't. It's just a strange feeling." Melody liked to be organized, but Belinda liked her things left out in the open. Mom always had to tell Belinda to put things away. The girls knew that they had not gone through all of the boxes yet, and that they would find everything within the next few days or so.

Suddenly, from down by the street, a young girl yelled over to Melody and Belinda. "Hi, I am your neighbor, you must be the new people," she said as she walked up to the porch. "My name is Sarah Cunningham. I live just a few houses down on the other side of the street." The girls introduced themselves and then sat and talked for a while. Sarah told them about the new school and found that she was the same age as Melody.

Then Melody asked Sarah about the Marshall mansion and told her about the waitress at the diner they had met the night before. Sarah explained about some of the strange things that happened at the mansion. People that would go to the mansion would come back pretty freaked out about it. They would make it just inside the front doors of the old house and decide to leave. There were only a few people that say they actually walked through the house, but declined to talk about it afterward. They just wanted to forget all about it. Most of the time kids would lie about going into the house, just to look brave. But it was still a mystery, and Melody felt an urge to find out more.

CHAPTER FOUR

Soon three months had passed, and the girls were already attending their new school. Stories about the Marshall mansion were adding up day after day. Everyone had a story to tell about the old place and how it was so haunted that no one wanted to go near it. As far as Melody was concerned, that is all it was… a story… but somehow she wanted to know more. She could feel the detective growing inside her. "Stories always seemed to get twisted around as the years go by, changing from one person to the next," she thought, one day she would find out the truth about the old abandoned house.

The bright warm sun beamed through the window where the fuzzy teddy bears and dolls sat on the window seat. Melody turned over clutching her pillow over her blue eyes, trying not to be blinded by the sun. It was Monday again, and she had to find the motivation to get out of bed and get ready for school. Today, she and her sister Belinda decided to walk to Danville Middle School rather than take the bus.

Melody pulled on her favorite pair of flared blue jeans and tie-dyed tee shirt, before heading to the bathroom to finish getting ready. She was tired of the butterfly clips and ponytails and decided to wear her dark brown hair down today. She could hear her sister yelling from the bottom of the steps to hurry. Melody ran from the bathroom and back into the bedroom to grab her backpack. She remembered that she had stuffed her mp3 player, headphones, and cell phone in her book bag the night before. There was absolutely no way that she could live through the day without those.

Melody was always cutting it close when it came to getting to school on time. She ran down the steps and into the kitchen to grab an apple. Then the girls yelled good-bye to their mother, who was in the kitchen cleaning up the morning dishes. Belinda grabbed her book bag from the front foyer and they started off to school.

Since Sarah Cunningham lived only a few houses away on the other side of the street, she would often meet up with Melody and Belinda at the corner. Sarah, like Melody, also had a curious streak that sometimes would get her in trouble. On the way to school, the girls would talk about exciting adventures they wished to encounter. The Marshall mansion was one of them, though each of the girls was a little apprehensive, they wanted to know what the house was all about.

The girls made it to school with little time to spare. They ran to their lockers to get a few things for their first class as the bell rang. Belinda was headed for her science class with Mr. Davidson, while Melody and Sarah went their own direction. On their way to class, Melody dug through her purse for her favorite cherry sparkle lip gloss and ran it quickly across her lips. Sarah and Melody would meet together with Belinda again at lunch.

Sitting in Mrs. Anderson's history class, Melody was daydreaming about what it was going to be like starting high school next year. Her sister Belinda was one year behind her and would probably end up in the same boring history class next year. Melody could never fully indulge the idea of history... it just didn't seem useful for her future, unlike her father, had always reminded her that it would be. Math maybe, but history never seemed to keep her attention. As long as she could get a decent grade and just get through it, Melody felt that was all she would need.

Only another twenty-two minutes and the bell would ring. Sarah sat in the next row of desks right across from Melody. They passed notes back and forth through most of the forty-five minutes the class lasted, trying to pass the time.

Melody looked over at Sarah who was in the process of writing a note and then looked forward at Mrs. Anderson.

"Hey Mel," Sarah said in a very quiet whisper.... then she tossed an intricately folded note over to Melody and then quickly looked forward at Mrs. Anderson to be sure that she had not been seen.

Melody quickly unfolded the note and began reading...

Mel,

What do you think about going to the Marshall mansion before winter sets in I think it would be a lot of fun to check out into all of those creepy rooms. Maybe we would be spooked out of our minds. We should ask Belinda what she thinks too.

w b

Sarah

They had written so much during class that there wasn't any space left on Sarah's note to reply. Melody leaned over the side of her desk and picked up her blue notebook and pulled out a clean sheet of paper from it. Thinking about going to the mansion was something she had thought about doing, but something kept changing her mind. She wanted to learn more about it before she went to investigate. The house had been vacant for many years and no one wanted to go near it. There were just too many strange stories circulating about the house being haunted. Melody began writing....

Sarah,

I have been thinking about the Marshall mansion since we moved here. I have always thought about going to see the house, but I'm still trying to get the nerve up. I will talk to Belinda, she will probably want to go. Sounds like a plan.

What do you think about Bob Mahoney? He is so cute...

w b

Mel

Melody folded the note and tossed it on Sarah's desk.

"How about you Melody, can you answer the question for me," Mrs. Anderson's said. Her voice was startling.

"Ah, no," Melody answered, feeling quite embarrassed and looked down at her desk, hoping everyone would forget quickly about how stupid she looked.

Soon the bell rang and Melody collected up her things and headed off to her locker with Sarah. They continued to talk about going to the mansion, and Melody told Sarah how it made her feel uneasy because of all of the stories. She was worried that she would freak out and call the whole thing off. She didn't want to let on that the whole idea did make her a little nervous. "But the thought of adventure was exciting," Melody told Sarah as they exchanged books at their lockers and made their way to the last class of the day. Sarah assured Melody that it would be a lot of fun to solve this mystery. Trying to change the subject, Melody asked Sarah again about Bob Mahoney. Sarah just shrugged her shoulders and smiled.

Sarah had lived in Danville all of her life and heard the stories about the old mansion over and over again. Talking about the mansion was easy, but the thought of going there made her uneasy as well. Sarah felt the same way that Melody did, but she didn't want to say anything. Just like Melody, Sarah also had a need to see the mansion and learn the real truth about it. She felt a need to keep Melody and Belinda interested in going to the house.

Sarah had a Math class and Melody was going to English, and they headed away in opposite directions. Sarah had a big test to take and she knew that she would have to concentrate. She needed to put the thoughts about the old mansion out of her mind until the end of the school day. Melody, however, could not stop thinking about it.

Melody entered the classroom as the last bell rang and settled into her chair. The thoughts of the mansion were now more intense then before. She just had to know more about the house and the family that once lived there. Stories had circulated for years since the house was abandoned. "What did people see that did make it inside the house?" Melody wondered. She began to feel a knot building in her throat. There seemed to be a strong need to go to that old house, but Melody was not sure why. "Maybe she was just making too much of the whole thing," she thought.

Melody's English teacher, Mrs. Marcel, paced back and forth in front of the blackboard, talking about the poetry homework from the night before. "Don't forget, you will need to bring in a mystery novel to be checked by me by tomorrow for you book reports," Mrs. Marcel announced.

Her voice seemed to be muffled and distant as Melody continued to think about the adventure they would soon encounter. "Sarah was right, it would be a lot of fun to solve this mystery. There was no way she would she allow fear to get in her way," Melody thought as her attention flashed back to what was going on in class.

Mrs. Marcel moved toward the front of her desk and faced the class. "Okay ladies and gents, I will give you the last ten minutes of class to start on your poetry assignment for tonight. Be as thorough as possible." Mrs. Marcel took one long look around the class and then sat down at her desk.

A list of requirements for the poetry assignment was written on the blackboard. Melody copied down the requirements for the assignment. Then she sat tapping her desk with the eraser end of her pencil, staring aimlessly at the wall. "Saturday might be a good day to go to the mansion," Melody thought to herself.

After a few minutes had passed, Mrs. Marcel looked up from her paper work and around the classroom. She noticed that Melody had been preoccupied during class time and still seemed to be in another world somewhere. Mrs. Marcel got up from her chair and walked over to Melody's desk. She put her hand on Melody's shoulder. Startled, Melody looked up at Mrs. Marcel. "Is everything alright today, you seem so far away during class?" Mrs. Marcel said, looking worried.

"Yes, I am fine Mrs. Marcel, just a lot on my mind," Melody replied, searching for something else to say. "I have just been thinking about the old Marshall mansion, I would like to know more about it."

Mrs. Marcel smiled and sat down in the empty desk in front of Melody. "You should go to the public library and check on it. If I am correct, it is quite an amazing piece of history." Mrs. Marcel continued, "Were you thinking of using it for your poetry assignment?"

"Yes... well, maybe I will," Melody said with uncertainty.

With that the bell rang, everyone rushed from their seats. It sounded like a herd of elephants racing to see who would be first to leave the room. What Mrs. Marcel had said about the library seemed like a good idea and Melody decided to take her advice. Maybe it would help her with the poetry assignment as well. It would also give them a head start on the Marshall Mansion.

Melody had to catch up with her sister to tell her about the plan to go to the mansion. She also wanted to let her know that she was going to go to the library after school.

She hurried down the hall right passed her friend Marcia who had been looking for her all day. Marcia was one of Melody's new friends, but Melody didn't seem to have much time lately to talk to her.

"Hey, Mel…wait up," Marcia yelled out.

Melody stopped and turned around to look at Marcia. Right away she remembered that Marcia had invited her to go camping with her family next weekend. They had a 31' travel trailer that they hauled to different parks during the year. This time they were supposed to go to Deer Lake. The thought of roasting marshmallows and telling ghost stories almost sounded better than going to the mansion. Melody had gone with Marcia's family to another campground a few times before and they made plans for this a couple of weeks ago. Marcia would be pretty upset if Melody broke her plans to go camping.

"Hey, how are ya?" Melody yelled back. Marcia caught up with Melody and they continued to walk.

Marcia could not believe that Melody had forgotten

their plans for the weekend. Melody explained about the Marshall mansion, and that it would be too cold pretty soon to go. Marcia understood about the weather, but couldn't believe that Melody was so set on going to the mansion. She knew that no one ever stuck around the old mansion for too long before high-tailing it out of there. Melody promised to go the following weekend and let Marcia know she would talk to her more about it tomorrow in school.

When Melody found Belinda, Sarah was with her. Sarah had already started to explain to Belinda about the plans to go to the Marshall mansion. Belinda seemed upset and shaken. She explained to Melody and Sarah that since they first learned about the mansion she started to feel as though something or someone was pulling her into going to the mansion. Belinda could not explain the strange sensation, but it seemed strong and was getting stronger the more they talked about the mansion. It scared her when she started hearing unexplained laughter in her head that no one else seemed to hear. Melody put her arms around Belinda trying to comfort her.

"Everything is going to be fine," Melody told Belinda, "You are probably just a little afraid of the unknown, and so are we. But think of the fun of the adventure!"

Belinda looked at Sarah and Melody and smiled. "You guys are probably right, I do feel a little nervous about the whole thing but I'll be fine," Belinda said, still trying to shake off the strange feeling she was having.

As they stood at Belinda's locker they saw Bob Mahoney. They realized that he knew he was gorgeous, but they stared as he walked by anyway. Snapping back to reality, Melody looked back over at Sarah and Belinda who still had their eyes focused on Bob as he turned the corner out of sight.

Regaining their attention, Melody explained what Mrs. Marcel had said about the library. They all agreed that Friday after school would be a good day to go to the mansion. Collecting information would take time and they all had to be home in time for dinner. With that, they all decided to go to the library together. Melody opened her purse, pulled out her cell phone and called her mother before they left for the library. Mrs. Drake told her that she would hold off on dinner and would have it ready at 6 o'clock to give them more time at the library.

CHAPTER FIVE

For early October the weather was still pretty nice, the temperature on the bank sign read 60 degrees as the girls walked along. A soft breeze blew through Melody's dark shoulder-length hair. The other two girls had their hair pulled back in long ponytails. Sarah and Belinda had worn light pull-over sweaters to school that morning and were comfortable in the cool autumn air. Melody, however, decided to pull the sweater from her book bag. The girls stopped for a moment while she slipped the sweater over her shoulders.

The library was a half block down the street, and they were just about there. During their short walk, they began planning their trip for Friday and decided that it would just be the three of them. They didn't want to mention their plans to anyone else. Melody and Belinda knew that their parents would almost certainly say no and forbid them from going to the mansion. Sarah knew her parents would feel the same, so they needed to come up with a plan that would work for all of them.

"What happened to you Mel, you freaked out twice on the thought of going and now you seem determined to go to the mansion?" Sarah chuckled. She loved picking on Mel because she took everything so seriously.

"I don't know, it almost feels like an investigation now. Maybe knowing more about the house is all I'll need to feel at ease. Besides, Friday seems so far off." Melody replied. "Well, if Mrs. Marcel is right, we should know a lot about the place before we get there," Belinda added.

The girls turned and walked up the sidewalk that led to the library. Melody pulled on one of the large brass door handles and they headed inside the library. The library was one of the largest historical sites in Danville. The girls stood in the large foyer at the entrance of the building and looked up at the tall beautifully constructed ceiling. A small brass plaque hung next to the double doors at the main entrance that read...

HISTORICAL LANDMARK

BUILT IN 1843

ORIGINAL SITE OF DANVILLE TOWN HALL

Sarah, who had been at the library many times before, looked down at her watch. It was already almost 3:30. She was no longer amazed by the essence of the old building and new that time was running short before they would have to get home for dinner. Sarah nudged Melody's arm, "we need to get going before it gets too late you guys," she said impatiently. With that Melody and Belinda followed Sarah into the main part of the library.

They began by searching through the card catalog. First they started with Danville's historical landmarks and worked from there. While the girls were searching, one of the librarians walked by and noticed that the girls were looking for information on the Marshall mansion. She guided them to a collection of old newspapers that the library had on micro-fiche. The library was still running on a lot of old technology, but had lots of good information.

There were bits and pieces of information on the family. Most of it seemed to be accumulated after the house was vacated in 1938. During the time that the family lived in the house, it talked mostly about the births that had occurred and a few articles on Mr. Marshall, who was an attorney. After 1938, most of the articles related to the strange things that people encountered while investigating the mansion and the property that surrounded it. Most of the articles leaned toward the fact that the house and property was haunted by the Marshall family.

The girls worked diligently, making copies of the most interesting articles. As they copied the information, Melody seemed to be more and more intrigued by the idea of going to the mansion. An interesting fact that caught the girl's eyes was the death of two of the Marshall children. The article stated that the children had just vanished without a trace. Also, there was a short article on their second born child, a girl, who had strange mental problems.

Melody and Sarah began the collect all the paperwork they had copied when they noticed that Belinda was pale and look ill. "Belinda, are you okay?" Melody asked. Melody and Sarah knelt down on the floor next to the chair Belinda was sitting on. "I guess I am okay," Belinda replied, "The room felt like it was spinning and I started to get a headache. I could hear that laughter in my head again and this time it sounded like a small child." With that, Belinda's stomach began to ache and she asked Melody and Sarah if they were ready to go home. Melody stuffed the paperwork in her book bag and they started walking toward the main entrance of the library.

Melody was becoming more and more worried about Belinda. Belinda had explained how she felt at school, and now here at the library she seemed even worse. First, Belinda felt like she was being pulled to the mansion and then the laughter and not feeling well. Everything seemed to be tied to the mansion in some way. Melody thought about how she had been feeling recently, and then brushed it aside. Belinda was much more important at the moment.

Many unexplained incidents happened at the mansion. The Marshall family was quite strange indeed the girls thought, and now Melody was even more determined then before. The house might be haunted like everyone talked about. Now Belinda was being affected by the whole thing and she wasn't anywhere near the old place.

As the girls walked home, Belinda seemed to be

feeling a little better. They stopped at Sarah's house for a few minutes to say good-bye before heading home. Melody and Belinda made it home just in time for dinner. They stepped inside the house and dropped their book bags in the main foyer. Then they went to join their parents who were already sitting at the dining room table. All through dinner the girls thought about their trip. Melody kept looking at her parents and wondering if they would go ballistic knowing what they were planning to do that following weekend. How would they react? Usually they were very understanding. This could be the big one that would not go over very well.

After dinner, Belinda was feeling much better. They went upstairs and finished their homework before calling Sarah. They needed to finish planning for their trip. They decided that Friday after school let out would be the best time to start on their way to the mansion. They needed to create a list of things they would need to take with them to the mansion. They didn't like lying to their parents and very seldom ever did. The plan they had come up with could get them grounded for what would seem to be the rest of their natural lives.

Belinda had come up with the idea to tell their parents that they were going to sleep over-night at Sarah's. Sarah would tell her parents that she would be sleeping over at Mel and Belinda's house. The plan seemed shaky, but simple enough. They would leave on Friday night and stay until Saturday afternoon at the mansion. They talked about the ghost stories that would feel more real than they had ever known. Ghosts that they could experience first hand! That is, if the house is really haunted. They all agreed and would set the plan in motion after school on Friday.

They proceeded to get ready for bed around 10:30... it would be a long week, Melody didn't think she could get to sleep knowing they would be lying to their parents like that. Belinda, however, was always asleep before the lights went out, and this night didn't seem to be any different.

That night Melody tossed and turned, dreaming about the old Marshall mansion. The house was cold and dirty, a sense of death was everywhere. In the dream, she felt as though there was someone watching her every move as she peered into each room. The house was huge with high ceilings and giant winding staircase that seemed to lead endlessly to the upstairs. As she moved up the stairs she could hear the wood beneath her feet creak and whine. At the top of the staircase was a large window made of stained glass. The wood frame of the window was curved at the top. Melody moved toward the window and looked out over what looked like a courtyard below. Suddenly, something touched her shoulder. Melody spun around... opened her eyes. Belinda was standing at her bedside.

"Come on Mel, wake up... we are going to be late for school," Belinda said, shaking Melody's shoulder.

"I'm up," Melody said in a low grumble, still half asleep... thinking about the dream.

Melody removed the crumpled blankets and swung her legs over the side of the bed and sat for a moment. Her thoughts of that vivid dream were still with her and a chill ran up her spine. She knew she was just overwhelmed by everything that was going on and that it would pass as soon as the day set in. Then she slowly got up and starting getting ready for school. She grabbed her purple book bag that seemed heavier than ever and headed downstairs to meet up with her sister who was already finishing her breakfast. Melody snatched an apple from the fruit bowl that sat in the middle of the dining room table. Then she and her sister ran out to catch the bus at the corner of their street.

The ride to school was only about twenty-minutes. Belinda, who was sitting with Sarah, noticed that her sister had not said a word since they got on the bus. All Melody did was stare out the window. Belinda was worried that she may have done something wrong and asked Melody if she was okay. Melody assured her that she was fine and that her mind was on the dream she had last night. She began to tell Belinda and Sarah about the dream and how real if felt. The only problem was that the dream wasn't leaving her like she thought it would.

Belinda was amazed by Melody's dream and moved from her seat with Sarah and sat next to her sister. "I had a dream last night as well, or at least I think it was a dream," Belinda said. "Last night I heard that child's laughter again, but it didn't seem like it was in my head this time. It was more real and intense than any time before. I looked around the bedroom to try to see who was doing it, but I didn't see anyone. But this time I am sure that it was a little boy that I was hearing."

Melody looked at Belinda, trying to understand the meaning behind the dreams they had. It was almost as though the house was calling them, or somehow giving them an idea of what it was all about. Sarah acknowledged that she didn't remember any dreams that night before. Maybe that was a good thing. Soon the bus pulled up in front of the school and the girls headed off to their first class.

It was already Wednesday, and the week seemed to be going by so slow. That entire day and the rest of the week Sarah, Belinda and Melody planned their weekend. Each of them was eager to see if Melody's dream was real, and maybe

meet the little boy that Belinda seemed to be hearing. Each of

the girls was excited about the adventure, and would be

amazed at what was about to unfold.

CHAPTER SIX

It was Friday, the day the girls had been waiting for was finally here. Melody grabbed the information she had on the mansion from the top of the dresser. She stuffed the pile of paper into her book-bag as she followed Belinda out the front door and on to the bus that was already waiting. Sarah was sitting toward the back of the bus waiting for them. They went over the list of things that they needed to take with them once more, making sure that they didn't forget anything. By that point the bus was pulling up to the school and the girls each went their separate way to their first class. They would meet up again in third period study hall.

Melody decided to try to set aside time to read over some of the information they had discovered at the library. She had not had all that much time during the past week with planning for the trip and homework. Getting a little more of an insight about the mansion would put her mind more at ease. During third period study hall the girls talked, and Melody didn't get a chance to read. The rest of the school day seemed amazingly long and busy.

Finally, they were on their way home from school. The girls pulled out the list of things they would need for the trip to the mansion. They went over it to make sure that they had not forgotten anything. Soon the bus came to a stop at the corner of their street. Melody, Belinda and Sarah got off the bus and hurried home to begin to set their plan in action.

They ran upstairs to Melody's bedroom and emptied their book-bags on the floor. They shoved all of their books and papers under the bed and began to collect things from around the house. They filled the bags with clothes, toothbrushes, rope, a flashlight, granola bars and sandwiches. Sarah would be bringing a small cooler with drinks and they would be all set to go.

The girls ran out to the back yard where their mother was doing some gardening. They let their mother know that they were leaving for Sarah's house. "Aren't you going to have dinner with us tonight," she asked Mel and Belinda. "No," they replied, almost at the same time. "We are eating with Sarah and her family tonight if it's okay..." Melody said, trying not to sound too anxious. Their mother nodded to them as they walked back to the front yard to get their bikes out of the garage.

Once at Sarah's, Melody and Belinda found a book bag and a small cooler sitting outside next to the back door. Belinda rang the doorbell. "Hold on you guys," Sarah said and came rushing out the door. "I left a note for my mom on the table reminding her that I would be at your house." Sarah opened the garage and grabbed her bike and the girls headed off down the road toward the Marshall mansion.

No one seemed to want to talk as the girls quickly pedaled down to the first stop sign. Only three more blocks and they would be out of their neighborhood and on to the main road. "It's off of this next side street," Sarah said. The girls guided their bikes down the side street and stopped for a moment to catch their breath. "It should only be a few more minutes before we get to the dirt road that leads to the house on Elm Drive," Sarah said as she sipped from her water bottle. The girls were tired from their ride and were glad that they were almost to the mansion. The ride so far felt like the long hallway that seemed to get longer as you continued to walk. Melody and Belinda stuffed their water bottles back into their book-bags, and the girls continued on down the road.

Their excitement grew more intense as they got closer to the mansion. Letting their imaginations to go wild, the girls talked about what they thought they would discover.

They knew that they needed to move along quickly if they wanted to get to the house before dark. The ride up to the dirt road that led to the house wasn't long, but once they turned down the dirt road they knew it would be awhile before they would reach the house.

Soon the road came to a dead end where there was a small sign that read, "Elm Drive." Belinda never believed in ghosts and was set on the idea that the house was not haunted. Even though she heard those strange unexplained voices, she thought that it was all her imagination. Or maybe she was willing herself to believe that. It was just supposed to be a scary old place that was abandoned for so long that people made up a bunch of stupid stories. The adventure she wanted was to find old treasures left behind by the Marshall family. She planned to look under every stone outside and behind every picture to find her treasure. Melody, however, didn't know what to think of the house. She had to see to believe. Haunted, that was possible she thought, but highly unlikely. And Sarah, she was along for the fun.

The girls rode along the edge of the road. Both sides of the road were heavily wooded. A small deer leaped out of the woods directly in front of the girls, stopped and looked at them, and then reentered the woods on the other side of the road. The road slowly curved and Belinda spotted what she thought was a tall white sign sticking up out of the under-brush.

"That must be it!" Belinda shouted out excitedly.

Sarah and Melody looked over to the right side of the road and saw a sign that was mostly covered with brambles and over growth. As they got closer they were able to get a better look. Belinda rode up close and got off her bike and began to carefully push the thorny stems that covered the sign to the side. After years of weathering the lettering on the sign was mostly worn off, but was still basically legible. The sign read...ELMWOODS...and in smaller lettering at the bottom... "Marshall Residence."

"I guess your right Belinda," Sarah said, staring at the sign. Sarah and Belinda looked over at Melody who stood straddling her bike, speechlessly looking down the dirt road that led to the house. Melody felt something strange like a weight in the pit of her stomach. Would she freak out again, she had almost made it to this point once before. "No," she thought to herself and swallowed hard, "we are going for it this time no matter what."

The trees that lined both sides of the long winding dirt road that led to the old Marshall Mansion, quivered in the mid-October breeze. Their branches arched over the road in an entangled embrace. Belinda and her sister Melody had planned their five- mile bike trip since the beginning of summer. This time they made it, they actually figured and had everything planned out... or so they thought. They had always heard all of the stories from kids in school about the strange things that happened at the Marshall mansion, but now they felt brave enough to check it out for themselves.

It was going to be fun to tell their own story about the mansion. They all felt that it was unlikely that the mansion was really haunted, but even if it were, it would still be a lot of fun. The girls started making up things that they thought would happen once they were inside the house.

Deciding that they needed to stretch a little after the long ride, they left their bikes leaning against the Elmwoods sign. Figuring that it wouldn't be too far down the road to the house, they started walking.

The sun had just started to set and the air started to get cooler. "I am glad we decided to dress warmly," Melody told her sister, her hands tucked deeply inside the pockets of her hooded fleece sweatshirt.

Sarah could feel a chill go up her back as they walked, "Me too, I wonder how far this road goes."

"From what I have heard, it is not too far, we should be seeing it soon," Melody said with a small shiver in her voice.

The girls kicked the fine dirt beneath their feet and watched the tiny dust clouds come up and then dissipate. "I know that I saw that rock twice before," Sarah said. Everything along the road started looking the same, as though they had been walking in circles.

"You're kidding around," Melody said.

"No, Mel, I've seen it before too," insisted Belinda, "I hope we are not walking in circles."

Suddenly, Belinda stopped and fell to her knees. She could feel what seemed like a pair of hands pressing down on her shoulders. Then a cold chill flashed through her. When she looked around to see who it was, there was no one there. She became pale and sick to her stomach. Melody and Sarah turned around to see what was happening. Belinda was still on her knees, her body bent over with her face cupped in her hands.

"Belinda!" Melody yelled…. "Are you okay? What happened?" Melody grabbed on to Belinda's arm and slowly brought her to her feet. Belinda started regaining the strength in her legs and stood straight up. Without saying a word, she looked around once more almost expecting someone else to be there with them. "I felt a little sick for a moment, but I am okay now," she replied, "something grabbed me by the shoulders and pushed me to the ground!"

Melody looked over at Sarah and then back at Belinda, "There is no one else here," Sarah said, feeling a bit confused.

The girls were going to turn back and head for home but Belinda encouraged them to continue on. Belinda just felt a little shook up. She could not see a reason to stop when they were almost there. Besides, whoever or whatever pushed her to the ground, seemed to be gone now.

The girls stopped and looked around, searching for anything else that seemed familiar. Nothing else caught their eye. Suddenly, a loud swooshing sound rushed through with the wind. Then a loud crackling from above their heads!

"Look out!" Melody said as a rush of adrenalin moved through her and she pushed Belinda and Sarah out of the way.

A giant tree branch broke off and fell directly in front of them. The three girls stood at the side of the dirt road and looked up.

"That was a close call," Belinda said as she brushed

leaves from her jacket sleeves.

"There are those who say this place is haunted... maybe this is just a small sign that it is. Maybe someone doesn't want us here," Sarah added, chuckling.

The middle of the dirt road was over-grown with grass and the tire-tracked parts of the path had almost disappeared. Thorny under-brush was growing into the path in bunches here and there, which the girls stepped over as they went along. The tree branches shuffled and crackled above their heads as they walked toward the mansion. The girls could only hope that they wouldn't encounter any more falling tree branches before they reached the house.

About twenty minutes from the road where they started the dirt road widened. They were amazed at how long it had taken them as they looked down at their watches.

It was just starting to get dark and a huge three-story white house stood before them. It looked like an old plantation home that they had seen in history books from the south. Thick ivy now draped the house from top to bottom and streamed down its huge pillars that seemed to give the house poise and stability. Six large windows that must have been eight feet tall, lined the first story of the house across its width. Tall black shutters framed the windows, one at each side. Two tall black doors stood in the middle of the face of the house. They opened from the center out and each had a long tarnished brass handle, just like the ones at the library. The front porch was littered with leaves and more of the thorny bushes that were growing from its edge. Small two-foot square slabs of stone formed the path that led from the dirt road to the front of the house. The girls just stood there motionless, looking at the house in amazement...

"Wow! Melody, everyone who has ever had the nerve to come here said this place is big, but it's enormous!" Belinda said with her eyes fixed on the third story windows above them. "I wonder how far people went when they got here, or if they chickened out and left right away. Maybe we will be the first to bravely conquer this adventure."

"The Marshall's built the house in the 1850's. The

Marshall family lived here until about 1938," Melody replied. "John and Ann Marshall came here from England and built the house. They seemed to be quite rich and had four children."

"C'mon, let's go you guys," Sarah said, pulling on Melody's jacket. "This is going to be great!"

CHAPTER SEVEN

Large flat topped stones lead onto the front porch. Over the years, grass had grown up around the stones and only a portion of each of them was visible. The girls began to make their way along the stone path onto the front porch. Suddenly, a large swoosh of wind encircled them, lifting the leaves off the ground and blowing their hair into their faces. At that very moment the large black doors didn't seem all that inviting.

The girls stood there for a minute, then Belinda decided to try the long curve-shaped handle on one of the doors. The door pulled itself from Belinda's hand and swung open and to the side. Being caught off guard, the girls stood at the opening for a moment looking through the doorway and then back at each other. They knew that they had just seen the door open on its own, seeming to be inviting them inside.

The three stepped cautiously inside the house. The foyer was large and had a strong musty odor. The floor looked like real marble, though most of it was covered with a thick layer of dust. A round table sat in the middle of the foyer with a candelabra sitting at its center. Thick webs swaged from candle to candle. The house was dark and only a small amount of natural light beamed through from the front door. Sarah reached inside the nap sack she had been carrying and pulled out a flashlight. She pointed the light around the room. A large chandelier hung down in the middle of the room, cobwebs swaying from its large intricate glass pieces.

There were two large arch-shaped openings that

stood on each side of the foyer and a curved staircase directly across from the front door. The walls were covered with a pale print paper that was faded and peeling and in some areas completely worn away. The girls walked over to one of the arch-shaped openings to the left of the front door and looked around. It seemed to be an enormous dining room with a fireplace at the far end of the room. The second arch-shaped opening revealed what looked like a living room. It had a massive stone fireplace on the far wall, nearly twice the size of the one in the dining room. Everything in the room was covered with white sheets. The girls walked back to the middle of the foyer and looked up the staircase. A long narrow hallway extended along side the staircase leading to the back of the house.

"Hey I don't know about you two, but I want to see more," Sarah said as she started down the narrow hallway. Belinda was not sure where to go so she decided to follow Sarah. The girls swung their arms above their heads, moving the cob webs that hung down from the ceiling.

The sun had now gone down and the house was completely dark. Melody opened her book bag and pulled out her flashlight and turned it on. She just stood there staring at the winding staircase in front of her. She thought about the dream she had, as she rested her hand on the dusty banister and looked up to the top of the stairs. Melody felt a sense of urgency to go further and started up the steps. The creaking of the steps beneath her feet were the same as in her dream, with an eerie whining sound. Melody stopped for a moment before continuing on to the top of the staircase. There she saw the large stained glass window that was curved at the top. "This is the same as the dream," Melody thought as she looked through the glass and saw a courtyard below her. "She remembered now, this was the point where Belinda had awakened her from her dream."

Suddenly, Melody heard a scream from very close by. She looked to her left, and then to her right. A hallway led away from her in each direction. Melody knew that there wasn't any way that Sarah or Belinda could possibly be upstairs. Then the thought occurred to her that maybe the main staircase wasn't the only passage to the upstairs, and Belinda and Sarah were playing a joke on her.

"Belinda...Sarah," Melody yelled...but no one answered. "Okay you guys, this isn't at all funny, where are you?" she said. Still no one answered and Melody could feel a chill go up her spine. She then turned and began to walk down the hall to the right of the staircase.

Melody slowly opened the first door that she came to and looked inside, her eyes scanning from one corner to the next. All of the furniture in the room was covered neatly with sheets just as it was in the living room. As she walked through the room she could feel a gentle cool breeze move around her. Curious, she unveiled one piece of furniture. It was a dresser with an oval mirror attached to its back. As she looked into the mirror she saw a shadow out of the corner of her eye that seemed to be moving. Melody turned to see what it was, but whatever it was had vanished. A moment later it happened again, but this time she caught the reflection in the mirror. Melody quickly turned to look and saw a black shadow move right through the door. Cautiously she walked over to the door and opened it... it was a closet... but the black shadow had disappeared again. Melody again felt cold. Rubbing her arms with her hands, she tried to fight off the chill. Slightly shaken by this, Melody closed the closet door and proceeded to go back to the hallway.

As Melody reentered the hallway she crossed her arms and rubbed the tops of her shoulders. The chill seemed to go through her and would not go away. Not wanting to run into the black shadow when she was by herself again, she decided to wait until the three of them were together. She wondered what had happened to Sarah and Belinda. With that thought in mind, she turned and headed back down the staircase where she had last seen them.

"Belinda...Sarah?" Melody called out and waited for a moment.

"BOO!" Sarah jumped out from around the corner.

"Are you trying to give me heart failure?" Melody

said, trying to get rid of the lump in her throat. "Have you seen Belinda?" She continued with a flutter in her voice.

"No, the last time I saw her was when we were all standing right here. I thought she was with you", Sarah replied, "But I thought I heard someone scream a little while ago and thought you guys were playing games."

"So did I, maybe we had better find Belinda," Melody said.

CHAPTER EIGHT

It seemed as though Belinda had just vanished, and after the screams Sarah and Melody had heard, they were beginning to feel uneasy. They wondered if Belinda was okay. Melody remembered that Belinda had gone off in the same direction as Sarah when they first had entered the house. Shining the flashlight around, Melody and Sarah walked through one of the large arched walkways from the foyer into the living room and looked around.

They began calling out for Belinda, but heard nothing. They moved on, down the hall along the staircase toward the back of the house, which was clearly the kitchen. Sarah walked to the back side of the kitchen. A set of doors with square glass panels from top to bottom led outside into the courtyard.

"Hey Mel, come here, look at this!" "I went another direction through the kitchen when I came through here the last time and ended up in the dining room. It is getting so dark in here that I didn't notice this the first time." Sarah said.

Melody walked over to the doors where Sarah was standing. When she looked out she could see the courtyard, but this time from the main floor of the house. It was huge and very overgrown. A large elm tree stood in the middle of the courtyard, its branches forming a type of canopy overhead.

By now dusk had set in, Sarah opened the door and they both walked out into the courtyard. "Maybe Belinda had come through here and found another passage." The girls thought.

The two girls searched around the courtyard. Directly across from the doors that led from the kitchen, was a path where two sides of the house were connected with a roof creating a small narrow passage way.

Walking down the path, they started yelling again for Belinda, but there was no answer. At the end of the path, the girls found themselves at the very back of the house. There was a small grassy area and the rest was thickly wooded. They continued to call out for Belinda, but could not hear or see anything unusual. Finally, they decided to turn around and walk back to the courtyard.

Melody and Sarah looked around the courtyard a second time, in hopes of finding a clue to Belinda's disappearance. All of a sudden they heard a screeching noise behind them. Both girls spun around to see where the noise was coming from. It was a cellar in the ground. One of the doors had fallen to the side and Belinda was climbing up out.

"Hey you guys, I wondered where you were,"

83

Belinda said, seeing the strange looks on Mel's and Sarah's faces. "I was looking for Sarah when I found this wine cellar, quite large too!" Belinda continued.

Melody was still wondering about the scream she heard when she was upstairs. "Hey Belinda, did you scream or hear any screaming since we all split up in the beginning?" Melody asked. "No, actually it has been very quiet the whole time, almost too quiet", Belinda replied.

The girls had to see the cellar that Belinda was talking about and walked down the wooden steps. Belinda was right, the cellar was large and it seemed to go on forever as Sarah shined her flashlight down the path in front of them. It looked like a large cave. The walls of the cellar were made of large stones set in mortar. About every five feet there were lanterns that lined the main isle. Belinda had lit the lanterns that lined the wide paths of wine racks.

Two large wood barrels sat in the middle of each of the isles. Sarah pulled a wine bottle from the rack and began to read it. "Some of the wine bottles are dated back to 1890 and 1873!" Belinda said with excitement in her voice. "This one says 1856," Sarah added, "The dates might even go back much further if the house was built in 1850."

Suddenly, Belinda felt something brush past her arm, blowing her hair up into her face.

"Wow, did you guys see that," Sarah said, her eyes lit up in the firelight. Though the torches on the wall lit up the area quite well, the far ends of the wine racks didn't receive as much of the bright light. Sarah guided the beam of the flashlight passed the ends of the wine racks to get a better look. Slowly she walked to the end of the isle. This isle ended into another that was going in the opposite direction. Sarah turned and stopped, and then started down the next isle.

"What?" Belinda said, a bit stunned and sick to her stomach. The queasy feeling was happening again, just like when they were in path leading up to the house.

"That," Sarah repeated as a black shadow passed at the end of the path they were standing in. It looked like someone dressed in a black hooded cape, but it seemed almost transparent with a white glow around it.

Sarah and Mel looked over at Belinda. Her face had gone pale and she looked ill. "Are you okay Belinda?" Melody asked. Belinda seemed to lose the strength in her legs and fell to the floor. Belinda looked up at Melody and Sarah, "I felt something brush my arm just before you saw that black shadow figure, and a strong cold chill went up my back," Belinda acknowledged.

"C'mon Sarah, help me stand her up," Melody said in a strong voice, "Are you going to be okay now Belinda?"

Belinda nodded, "I think so."

"I saw something like that black shadow in one of the upstairs bedrooms just a little while ago," Mel said, "It disappeared into a closet, but when I looked in the closet there was nothing there."

The girls walked down the path and looked around the corner. The black shadow was about three isles ahead of them and turned the corner. The girls ran to keep up, but as they came up on the shadow, it disappeared into the wall. As soon as the black shadow disappeared, Belinda began to feel better.

Not sure what they had seen; Mel, Sarah and Belinda decided to hurry out of the cellar. The whole place seemed to be a maze of wine racks and isles going everywhere. Unsure of which way to go next, the girls frantically searched for a way out. Finally finding the entrance, they swiftly ran up the steps and slammed large wood doors behind them.

"What was that thing?" Belinda said, hunched over with her hands on her knees.

"I don't know you guys, but I get the feeling that won't be the last time we see it," replied Melody.

"I don't know either, I just want to stop shaking," said Sarah, "this place is creepy."

CHAPTER NINE

Still a little shaken the girls went back into the house. Knowing that it was starting to get late, Belinda looked at her watch, but it didn't seem to be working. She tapped the face of the watch a couple of times and looked again. "Hey, you guys, my watch stopped," Belinda said. The other two girls looked at their watches.

"Looks like ours stopped as well," Sarah said. That seemed like quite a strange coincidence they all agreed.

The girls wondered what that black shadow figure was, could it be a ghost that they didn't want to believe in? It was transparent, not to mention the white glow that surrounded it. All they could do was guess. Besides, what else could go into a closet and disappear or walk into a wall and vanish? It didn't seem to be harmful, maybe it was just as curious as they were. In any case, they decided to stick closer together.

"I am feeling a bit hungry," Belinda said. Melody and Sarah agreed. The girls stopped and sat down on the steps and began to go through their bags. They ate their sandwiches that they brought along and relaxed for a while.

They talked about the black shadow and wondered what else they might find, and the sickness that Belinda felt every time something happened. The first time she felt sick was in the path leading to the house when the tree branch fell, and then in the cellar when the black shadow appeared. She seemed fine as soon as the shadow disappeared. They couldn't figure out what was making Belinda sick for those short intervals, and then fine again, as if nothing had happened at all. It was, however, becoming quite obvious that her sick spells had to do with the house.

Finally the girls moved off into the living room. They pulled some of the sheets from the furniture and sat down to talk for a while longer. The house felt cold and damp and the girls had a strange feeling that someone was watching them. A small cradle of wood sat near the opening of the fireplace and Sarah walked over and started a small fire. Then she walked back to the couch and sat down with Mel and Belinda. They decided to make some fun out of all the things that had happened and tell a few jokes and ghost stories. Nothing seemed to make the strange feelings they were having go away.

Suddenly, Melody woke up; she and the others had not realized that they had fallen asleep and it was now daybreak. "Wake up you guys!" Melody said, shaking Belinda and Sarah. They opened their eyes and squinted around the room.

"What happened?" Sarah said dazed. "We must have fallen asleep here last night, and I don't recall anything." Melody replied. None of the girls could recall what had happened last night and time seemed to pass so quickly.

Small puffs of smoke were all that was left of the fire they had started the night before. The girls sat for a while until they felt more coherent. Light was pouring in the front windows of the living room from the morning sun. Melody had just suggested that they continue looking upstairs, when there was a crashing noise above them on the second floor.

CHAPTER TEN

"That sounded like it came from upstairs," Belinda
said. The girls looked at each other and then headed for the
front of the house and ran up the staircase to the second floor.
A tall wooden stand stood in the corner at the top of the steps.
A large glass vase that once was perched there had fallen to
the floor.

"Maybe there is someone else in the house," they
thought. Maybe that is why they kept feeling like they were

being watched, but not one of them wanted to acknowledge that they felt that way.

There were seven doors on the second floor, three on one side of the staircase to the left and four to the right. Each of the girls went to different doors that lined the hallway on the left side of the main staircase. They cautiously opened them one by one carefully looking around.

"Oh my God, come here you guys," Sarah said as she stood in the doorway of one of the rooms, her face as white as freshly fallen snow.

Both Melody and her sister ran down the hall to see what was going on. The room was hazy, but they could see what looked like a little girl sitting on the bed. The figure of the little girl seemed to slightly disappear in the haze. The little girl just sat there with her legs kicking lightly back and forth on the side of the bed. She wore a green flowered dress and a pair of shiny black shoes, her blonde hair tied back in two braided ponytails. Sarah, feeling a little more courageous, took a deep breath and slowly took three steps closer to the little girl.

"What is your name?" Sarah asked in almost a whisper.

The little girl looked up at Sarah with a blank look on her face. "Laura, my name is Laura," the little girl replied, tears rolling down her face.

"What's wrong" Sarah asked Laura. Her friends stood behind her and listened. Melody and Belinda noticed that Laura didn't seem to be whole. Just like the black shadow, Laura seemed to be transparent, and appeared to be fading in and out. At one point she looked as though she was disappearing. This was absolutely crazy to think that Sarah was talking to a ghost! Now it seemed more convincing than ever that they had seen and talked to ghosts!

"I have been looking for my friend Jimmy, and I can't find him," Laura replied sniffling, "Maybe you can help me find him?"

"Of course we will help you," Sarah said as she looked back at Mel and Belinda.

Again, Belinda had begun to feel ill, but this time it didn't seem as bad, and she decided to keep it to herself. "Being ill one time too many and Melody would insist that they leave and go home," Belinda thought. Belinda now expected to feel ill when ever they came across one of the entities or ghosts… or whatever they were. Besides, the adventure was becoming more and more exciting. As long as she didn't feel too ill, she wanted to continue searching the house.

Laura stood up, but her feet didn't seem to be touching the floor. Then she motioned to Sarah, Melody and Belinda to follow her. Then Laura led the girls out of the bedroom, down the staircase. All along she hovered a few inches from the floor, her feet and legs not moving. When Laura reached the front door, she just passed right through it! Amazed by what they had just seen, Sarah opened the front door and the girls continued to follow Laura.

Laura led them around the side of the house to the back yard. They entered the woods that were about a hundred feet from the house. They followed Laura down a narrow over-grown path for quite a while. After about ten minutes they came to a clearing. The breeze blew across the grass like the waves in an ocean. A short distance away the girls could see a lake which glimmered in the sun's rays. Laura seemed to glide across the open field ahead of the girls. She guided them to the far side of the lake under a giant oak tree.

"Jimmy and I kept a secret diary that we have buried right here by the tree under this rock," Laura said. "We collected many things which we put with the diary and hid them inside a wooden box. Some of the things belong to my parents and need to be returned to them. I am unable to do this on my own, that is why I need your help," Laura continued. Then Laura, seeming very sad, looked out over the lake and pointed. "Jimmy went in right here, and he never came back out," she said, tears pouring from her eyes. "I really tried to save him, I truly did!"

The girls looked at each other, not knowing what to say as they watched Laura glide out over the water. The tips of her shoes were skimming the top of the water, and then she vanished into thin air.

"This just isn't real," Sarah thought…"no one… nothing could do what we just saw. We must be dreaming." First the black shadow and now Laura; maybe the mansion was really haunted and they really did see ghosts. They truly could not ignore the idea any longer. Maybe everything people said about the mansion was true. What would they encounter next? Only time would tell. Maybe the diary would give more of an indication of what they would look forward to.

Melody looked over at Belinda who was looking a little pale. "What did we just see?" Melody said, "I hope we didn't just imagine all of that."

"I am not sure Mel, and I don't want to go home, but the longer the encounter, the more ill I feel," Belinda replied, feeling a bit stunned.

"Oh, come on Belinda, this is just getting exciting," Sarah added, "This is great, you have to admit!" Belinda, beginning to feel a little better, agreed with a bit of uncertainty.

"I am enjoying the adventure too, I am just trying to cope with my stomach and my head spinning," Belinda said.

While they were talking, Melody picked up a big stick that was lying close to the tree. She moved the rock aside and began to dig up the ground where Laura had said the diary was buried. Scraping at the ground inch by inch and then, she hit something. She scraped just a little bit more. About eight inches down was a small wooden box! "Look you guys, I've found the wooden box!" Melody said, excited to see what was inside.

Belinda and Sarah waited patiently and watched as Melody used the stick and dug around the box to loosen it from its resting place. Finally she was able to remove the box from the hole. Then she went over to the edge of the lake and washed her hands.

The box was about eight inches long, six inches wide and a couple inches deep. It was covered with a layer of thick dirt from being in the ground for over fifty years. Sarah picked up the box and scraped off some of the dirt around the lock. Then she tried to open it, but it was locked. She pulled her nap sack from her back and began searching for the pocketknife she had taken from her brother's room before she left. Picking at the lock for a moment, Sarah popped the lid open.

Inside the box was the diary that Laura had mentioned. The girls skimmed through the diary for a short time before coming across something quite interesting. It was a heart shaped locket stuck in the binding of the diary. Inside the locket was a picture of Laura and an older woman who might have been her mother.

Belinda glanced down at her watch, forgetting that it didn't work. She was feeling tremendously tense and wanted to move along, even if it meant going back into the house. Belinda thought for a moment, now she was sure of her feelings. Something or someone did seem to be pulling her back to the house. She now had an overwhelming urge to get moving, but she didn't want to let on to Sarah and Mel how she felt.

Sarah opened the box and was about to put the diary back inside when she saw six clear-shiny stones on the bottom. "They look like diamonds! " Sarah said as she held up one of the stones. Each of the girls picked up one of the glimmering stones and looked closely..."maybe they are diamonds!" the girls all agreed. "The locket and the diamonds must be what Laura wanted to be given back to her parents," Melody said, "but how are we supposed to give them back.... to ghosts?" They put the stones and the diary back in the wood box and put it in Sarah's book bag.

Melody sat back against the tree and thought for a moment about the notes that they had copied down at the library. Now she remembered Laura... and began to explain it to Belinda and Sarah. Laura used to go fishing with her father at this lake during the summers. One day, while playing with her friend Jimmy, they drowned in the lake. Laura was only twelve years old. Laura must have been looking for Jimmy in the lake when she drowned as well. Now, after all of these years, she is still searching for him. It must have been a strong friendship for Laura to do what she did.

Trying to get back to reality, they knew the day was going by fast, and Belinda had been hinting on the idea of going back to the house. If they wanted to see any more of the house, they would have to get going. The girls knew it was getting later in the morning and they needed to get back on their way to the house. On their way they snacked on granola bars that Melody had brought along for the trip.

CHAPTER ELEVEN

During their walk through the woods the girls could not shake the thought of Laura and decided to stick as close together as possible. Belinda, unable to explain it, felt the pain that Laura was going through and felt sorry for her. Too many strange things had happened already and they weren't going to take any chances. Belinda was feeling a little better about continuing the investigation of the house. As for Melody and Sarah, the excitement grew stronger inside them.

The girls decided that they needed to read more into Laura's diary to get more insight into what had happen with Jimmy and the Marshall family. The house was soon in sight and the girls decided to walk around and enter through the front door. Belinda felt strongly about avoiding a short cut through the courtyard.

Sarah walked through one of the large arched walkways that led to the living room, or parlor, which is what they were called in the old days. Melody and Belinda followed and the three sat down on the floor in front of the huge stone faced fireplace. They began to read the diary. Laura had written a few short passages, which seemed to be on the day of the drownings. They found that Jimmy was not Laura's best friend, but her adopted brother. This made more sense as to why Laura seemed to be so close to him. Maybe because he was adopted, she considered him her best friend.

Unexpectedly, the girls began to feel the house shutter, almost like a small earthquake. Slowly the shuttering became more of a violent shaking! The windows rattled and small objects that sat on a bookshelf in the corner fell to the floor. Melody, Belinda, and Sarah, who had been sitting on the floor, all jumped to their feet and grabbed each others hands. They began looking around the room. Suddenly, with a powerful sweeping blast, a large fire started in the fireplace. The girls ran for the foyer. Then about as quickly as it all started, the shaking stopped and the fire was now just a small flame that was slowly dying out.

"Are you guys okay?" Sarah said, still holding her friends hands.

"I think so," Melody said as she looked at Belinda.

Belinda's hands were cold and clammy, her face flushed with fear. "They want something from us, I can feel it," Belinda said. Her heart felt like it had jumped to her throat making her feel like she was choking. Melody took Belinda and sat with her sister on the couch.

"How do you know that they want something from us and who wants it?" said Melody. She tried to reassure Belinda who now just sat there trembling violently. The look in Belinda's eyes was horrifying. She sat not saying a word and not moving. "Belinda?" Melody said, but Belinda just sat motionless. Suddenly Belinda just snapped out of it... "What happened?" she said.

"You just sat there in a trance, mumbling something about they want something from us...do you know who?" Melody asked.

"Well I feel okay now," Belinda said, "the house started shaking and I don't remember anything else. "I feel like it is the parents that want something and they want us out of here." Belinda tried to get it out of her mind and proceeded to get up from the couch. Melody watched Belinda pace back and forth, wondering if the things that Laura wanted them to give to her parents was what they wanted. Maybe Laura's parents already knew about the locket and the diamonds. Now the question was, how would they give her parents the locket and diamonds?

Sarah walked over to one of the tall windows and looked out, trying to figure out everything that had just happened.

"Come on you guys... we've come this far and nothing happened that hurt us in any way. I know we can go on from here." Melody said, looking in her sister's eyes and trying to be encouraging.

In the back of Melody's mind she kept thinking about how her parents would feel if they knew they had not stayed the night at Sarah's house. What if her parents found out what they had really done? It was already too late to worry about that, and they needed to go and finish what they had started. Mel looked back at Belinda, wondering if she would get through the rest of the adventure.

Belinda nodded, "Okay, let's do this," she said.

Sarah walked over to Belinda and put her hand on Belinda's shoulder.

The girls knew there was more investigating to be done on the second floor. Melody stood up from the couch and followed Sarah and Belinda through the arched walkway and up the staircase. As they looked to their left down the hallway, it looked distorted. The walls and floor seemed to be moving, like liquid in a glass, and then suddenly it stopped. The girls stood there for a moment and then slowly began walking down the hall.

CHAPTER TWELVE

A loud shrieking sound came from behind a closed door at the end of the hall. Melody gradually moved toward the door and started to turn the knob. With a small screeching sound the knob turned and Melody stepped inside. Sarah and Belinda waited for only a few seconds before following Melody inside the room.

Just like all of the other rooms they had seen, all of the furniture was covered. Melody began to uncover one piece of furniture at a time while her sister and Sarah did the same. Sarah pulled a sheet off a picture on the wall uncovering a painting. "This must be Mr. Marshall," Sarah said. His blue eyes seemed to glare back at Sarah, watching her every move.

The girls moved on and uncovered the rest of the furniture in the room. It had a desk with a comfortable high-back chair. Bookcases lined the wall on one side of the room and on the opposite side were two large windows that looked out into the woods.

Mr. Marshall's eyes continued to follow Sarah as she moved around the room. She told herself over and over again that pictures could not see and that she was imagining the whole thing. To ease her tension, Sarah began thinking about the movies she had seen. She moved over to the picture of Mr. Marshall and moved it aside to see if there was a vault behind it. Nothing was there of course, but the adventure was fun and she was curious.

Melody sat down at the desk and looked inside a few

of the drawers but found only a few scraps of paper, a few files, and an old pen. As Melody opened the last drawer at the bottom she saw a photograph and pulled it out to show Sarah and Belinda. It looked like a family picture, in black and white and quite worn and faded. It showed Mr. and Mrs. Marshall and all four of the children. It must have been taken just after they adopted Jimmy. Mr. Marshall looked just like his picture that hung on the wall with the same peering blue eyes.

In the bookcases along the wall the girls found Law and Real-estate books. Judging from some of the files Melody found in the desk drawer, it seemed that Mr. Marshall was a very busy attorney and probably a very good one to be this rich. He must have dealt in real estate dealings in his free time the girls thought.

After searching for clues in the study the girls decided to move on down the hall to the last room. As they left the room, Sarah looked again at the picture of Mr. Marshall. His eyes were following them, and now she knew that she was not imagining anything. Not saying a word to the others, Sarah quickly moved out into the hall and closed the study door behind her.

Going to the next room, it seemed to be the only room that they had not investigated on this end of the hallway. They stood still in front of the closed door and then turned and looked at each other. Belinda slowly turned the knob and opened the door only a few inches to peek inside. She could feel her stomach turn and her head throb with extreme pain. "Not again," Belinda thought as she stepped back into the hall.

It was another bedroom, quite a bit larger than the others. Sarah pushed the door the rest of the way open until it bumped the wall with a slight thud. "This must be the master suite," Sarah said with a pronounced accent. She took two small feminine steps into the room and made a half turn toward Melody and Belinda. "You may enter," she said as she made a slight bow and waved her arm through the air.

There was a strong smell of sweet perfume that filled

the air as the girls walked to the middle of the large room. A big four-post bed stood against the wall in the center of the room. There were leaf pedals intricately carved into each of the posts. An arched canopy made of lace and fine linen connected to each of the posts and hung lazily over the bed. Cobwebs hung from the canopy down to the bed. Melody anxiously observed the room while her sister, Belinda, stood quietly trying to ease the pain she was feeling.

Unlike the other rooms, only a small portion of the furniture was covered with sheets. The girls began to remove sheets which they stacked neatly in the corner behind the door. The entire room was filled with ornate objects such as vases and small knick-knacks. An enormous armoire stood off on its own in the far corner. Belinda, struggling not to show any pain, opened the large doors of the armoire to reveal what was inside. An odor of moth balls flooded the room, quickly mixing with the strong scent of sweet perfume. About a dozen black men's suits were hung neatly from above. Belinda pushed the clothes out of the way to see what was in the bottom of the cabinet. She found a small wood box hidden among the neatly lined pairs of shoes.

Belinda bent down and picked up the box. She opened it and found that it was filled with small trinkets, tie clips and cuff links. "Mr. Marshall seemed to be the type of guy that was dressed up nicely each and every day," she thought as she closed the lid of the box and placed it back in its original resting place. As Belinda proceeded to close the large cabinet, Melody screamed and jumped back away from the dresser where she had been looking through the dusty jewelry that lay on its top.

Sarah, who had been looking through the closet, ran over to Melody.

"What happened?" Belinda said as she walked over to join them.

Sarah, who was still shaken from what she saw in the study, knew that they were still being watched. The feeling was stronger now then ever and it sent a chill up her back. She felt as though she was coming unraveled and needed to pull herself back together so that the others would not notice.

"I don't know," Melody replied feeling slightly unnerved. "I was just going through a few pieces of jewelry and when I looked up at the mirror, there was a woman looking back at me! At almost the instant that I saw her, she vanished. I think it was Mrs. Marshall!"

Suddenly the odor of perfume that was present when the girls first entered the room became overwhelmingly strong. It was like a blanket in the air that was choking them. "We need to get out of here now!" Sarah said as she pushed her friends out into the hall and closed the bedroom door. The girls stood coughing in the hallway and then looked back at the bedroom door. It was almost like Mrs. Marshall wanted them out.

"That certainly was a strong message," Belinda said as she took a deep breath. "Do either of you feel as though we have been watched ever since we entered this house?" Belinda asked.

Melody and Sarah were both convinced that someone

was watching their every move. "I also saw Mr. Marshall's eye's following us around the room when we were in his study earlier," Sarah added.

The girls agreed that it was time to move on and try to ignore the strange feelings they had. They decided to move on to the opposite side of the main staircase and check out the last couple of rooms.

CHAPTER THIRTEEN

For the next half hour nothing happened out of the ordinary. Belinda had finally gotten rid of the pain in her head and stomach. Maybe there was nothing else haunting about the house and they could just go room-to-room and check things out. That would be fine with them. The shrieking noise they heard before when they opened the door to Mr. Marshall's study was the only thing they could not explain.

Finding nothing else, they moved on to the next room down the hall going toward the staircase. Nothing seemed out of the ordinary in this room or in each of the next two rooms they looked into. One seemed to be a child's room and the other was set up like a sewing room, which must have belonged to Mrs. Marshall.

Sarah looked over at Melody and reminded her that they had not checked the attic. The three decided to sit down at the top of the steps and munch on some chips they had brought along and relax a bit before going to the attic to explore further. Melody, who was always on a diet, brought along a bag of carrot sticks and bottled water, which was now pretty warm from sitting in the book bag. They sat and talked for a while after finishing their snack. Since their watches weren't working, they could only guess that it was about one o'clock or so in the afternoon. Before the sun set they wanted to finish investigating the house and start heading toward home.

Next to the main staircase, but going in the opposite

direction, there was another set of steps that lead to the third floor attic. The girls got up from the main staircase and walked over to look up the stairs. The railings that lined the steps were coated with a thick lining of dust, as were the steps that led to the attic floor above. Belinda removed her hand from the railing and wiped some of the dust off onto her jeans. The three girls followed each other single-file to the top and looked around. Boxes and old dusty furniture sat unorganized from one end to the other of the large attic, which seemed to expand the entire length and depth of the house.

Sarah found an old trunk and started wiping the dust away with her hand to get a better look at it, she then lifted the lid. Just like in the Marshall's bedroom, the aroma of sweet perfume and mothballs suddenly became apparent again.

Trying to ignore the smell, Melody joined Sarah and they started going through some of the old trinkets, photographs, and clothing in the trunk. There were some trinkets that were ornate but beautiful that Mrs. Marshall had kept hidden in a small box toward the bottom of the trunk.

In the bottom of the trunk they also found a dress. Melody pulled the dress out of the trunk and held it up in front of her. She walked over to a mirror that was leaning against the wall. The dress was astonishingly beautiful. It had tiny white beads that looked like pearls sewn in a diamond pattern all over the dress. There was a white lace veil that matched the dress. This must have been Mrs. Marshall's wedding dress. It was absolutely breath-taking. Melody and Sarah continued to look for more clues that would tell them about the Marshall family. Under the box of trinkets, Sarah found a diary. As she opened it, she found that it too belonged to Mrs. Marshall.

By this time the smell of perfume and mothballs was again becoming overwhelming. Sarah closed the diary and stuffed it in her nap sack. Melody quickly put the wedding dress and small trinkets back in the chest and slammed it shut.

Belinda was still feeling uneasy about being at the

house. She walked over to the window and looked out over the driveway below. Something was noticeably odd about it... it looked very different from when they first arrived at the house. Things looked new and perfectly trimmed. The brambles and thorny bushes they had encountered during their walk to the house were gone and the driveway wasn't overgrown. She called Mel and Sarah to the window where she was standing.

"Look at this you guys, it's all changed," Belinda confirmed.

Mel and Sarah looked out the window in amazement. It had all changed, something was happening, but what? Behind them they could hear a whipping sound and turned only to see a mist of dust lifting into the air. The furniture, curtains and floors were free of dirt and dust! It was like the clock was turning back and the house was changing back to its original shape. Maybe the way it looked when the Marshall's had lived in the house. The girls just stood there watching in astonishment as things began to move about the room and change. A chair gently moved by itself to a new resting place against the wall. Papers and small objects gracefully lifted themselves off the floor and moved around the room. They settled in what seemed like their original positions of over fifty years ago!

Without another thought the girls ran down the first flight of steps to the second floor and looked in each of the rooms. The white sheets had vanished and everything was perfectly clean. As they walked back to the staircase that led to the main floor they could see the glimmering marble floor in the foyer. They noticed the air was no longer musty, and the strong smell of perfume and mothballs was slowly clearing from the air. The whole house looked new and beautiful again!

This just wasn't possible, Melody thought as she followed her sister and Sarah to the foyer. Even the wallpaper that was torn and faded was like new again. The girls walked out on to the front porch and into the driveway. They turned and looked up at the house. All of the ivy streamers had vanished… was the house going back in time?

Sarah walked back into the house and stood in the foyer, her friends followed shortly after. Belinda also seemed to be changing. She now seemed more intrigued about the house, like she too had gone through a change with the house. She seemed so much more comfortable and acted as though she had been there all of her life.

"Are you alright?" Melody asked Belinda.

Belinda turned and looked at Melody, "Yes, I am perfectly fine," and she began walking up the steps back to the second floor, turned the corner and disappeared down the hall.

Sarah and Melody were confused about Belinda's change in attitude about the house, and with all of the changes, she didn't seem ill. For most of the day she wanted to just go home and seemed not to be feeling well. Now she had changed suddenly and they did not understand why. She most certainly was not acting like herself. Before they knew it there was a short creaking sound and the front door slammed shut behind them. Mel looked at Sarah and then at the front door, then ran up the stairs to find Belinda.

CHAPTER FOURTEEN

Melody and Sarah went upstairs to the second floor and began searching from room to room trying to find Belinda. They could hear screams coming from one of the rooms toward the end of the hall, but they weren't sure which room. As they walked passed the second door to the left of the main staircase, they heard the screams again. They stopped at the door for a moment, listened, and then opened the door. As they opened the door and looked in there was an older girl standing at the foot of a large four- poster bed with a curved lace canopy top.

Hundreds of snakes covered the floor and were crawling over the girl's feet. Melody and Sarah stood in the doorway, not sure what to do next. She screamed again, leaping from one foot to the other, trying to avoid the snakes. Jumping over the piles of these horrible creatures, the girl ran for the set of light switches next to the closet door. She began switching them up and down with both hands, but the lights would not work. Her screams became brutal and high pitched. Frantically the girl tried the knob on the closet door, but it would not open. Suddenly, the tangled pile of snakes that were once there had vanished. She tried the lights again to no avail.

Melody and Sarah watched the girl as she stared, in a trance like state, at the closet door in front of her. Her eyes set and focused, as though she were dreaming. This ghost looked more real than the others Mel and Sarah had encountered so far. She seemed to be more solid, her cries not washed out by time. Then she walked back across the floor toward the middle of the room. Silently she paced in front of the bed a few times, and then stopped and continued to stare at the closet door. It was almost as though see was afraid to go inside the closet.

Now that the snakes had disappeared, Sarah decided to walk up to the girl. "It's okay," Sarah told the girl. She stood in front of her and put her hands on the girl's shoulders and looked into her eyes. Streams of tears came from the girl's eyes and she quivered in fear.

"What's wrong?" Sarah asked

The girl shook, her cries becoming stronger. Then she opened her mouth, but no sound came from her lips. Then in a terrified gulp she cried out....

"There coming to get me!" she screamed, "tried the lights, but nothing works, and the snakes.... the devils... they're coming to get me!"

"The snakes are gone," Sarah reassured her, "See, look!" The girl turned in a circle looking all around the room.

"They are gone, but they will be back," the girl cried out.

"Who is coming to get you?" Sarah asked, not sure if she had heard the girl right the first time. The girl looked at Sarah with horrible fear in her eyes. Sarah began to wonder if she should have asked at all.

"The devils... they chased me here!" she cried, still staring at the closet. "Even if I lock the door, they can still get in, nothing can stop them!"

Sarah tried to calm the girl, sitting her down at the edge of the bed. "Devils don't exist," Sarah tried to explain to the girl. Melody, still standing in the doorway, watched in amazement. Sarah found out that the girls name was Ashley and that she was fourteen years old. Sarah looked over at Melody and motioned for her to come over by the bed. "This is Melody, and my name is Sarah. Will you walk with us over to the closet door?" Ashley nodded slowly and then stood up and started to walk towards the closet. Melody reached for the door knob.

"No! Don't go in there!" Ashley shouted, her large eyes beaming at them. "That's where the devils come from!"

"We won't let anything or anyone hurt you," Sarah told Ashley in a calming voice.

Ashley shook with fear as Melody turned the knob on the closet door. This time the door opened. Melody decided to try the lights, but they still would not work. There was a sliver of sunlight coming into the bedroom. Melody backed off and Sarah looked inside… they didn't see anything out of the ordinary. Just some clothes that hung neatly on their hangers and a few items on the shelf above.

"They come out of the floor!" Ashley pointed.

Sarah looked down at the closet floor only to see a small hole. She stuck her finger in the hole and pulled the small door open. It was a small door, fashioned of wood. It was approximately 2' x 3' with two hinges on one end holding it in place to the floor. Sarah swung the door back and rested it against the wall of the closet.

"Hey look Mel…. It's a trap door to a passage down

below the floor!" Sarah said in excitement. As Sarah looked down through the hole in the floor she could feel a chill, the hair on her arms stood straight up. Her mind started racing as she thought about going down into the dark passage. They could get trapped down there, and what if the devils that Ashley talked about really did exist? They needed to find Belinda and it seemed that this was their only choice. They needed to search below the floor and see what was down there. Sarah knew that she was letting her fears get the best of her.

Melody and Sarah turned to ask Ashley where the passage in the floor led, but she had vanished. Sarah ran over to the bedroom door and looked up and down the hall, but there was no one. She walked back over to the closet where Melody was sifting through her book bag for the flashlight. "Did you see Ashley?" Melody asked.

"No," Sarah replied, "she's gone!" Melody pointed the light from the flashlight down the hole in the floor of the closet. Sarah yelled down into the hole, she could hear her echoing voice fade out far away. "You do know that this is really not making any sense at all..." Melody said, "Isn't the living room below us?"

As Sarah and Melody stood looking into the hole in the floor, a little boy ran up to the bedroom door. Hopping in circles, he entered the bedroom, grabbed the knob and slammed the door. He was laughing as he ran across the bedroom floor toward the window, and then vanished into thin air. Melody and Sarah were quite amused by the little boy. Melody began to wonder where he played into all of this.

Melody thought about the Marshall children. She knew that there were four. They had already encountered Laura, Jimmy, and Ashley; and the little boy that just vanished must be Johnny.

This is way too weird the girls thought. Maybe he was the one that slammed the front door a short time ago when they were standing in the foyer downstairs. He seemed innocently playful and Melody and Sarah were not afraid of him, just astonished by his appearance.

They looked back down into the passage. One side had what looked like a tree trunk with pieces of wood nailed to it like steps, just like a ladder going to a tree house. Melody and Sarah were unsure of what to do first. "Maybe we shouldn't go down there," Sarah said with a quiver in her voice.

"We have to find Belinda and we have to check this out," Melody replied, "pull yourself together and let's go!"

Melody decided to pull the long rope from her book bag. She tied one end of the rope to a heavy piece of furniture in the room and the other end she tied around her waist. Then she turned with her back to the hole, got down on her hand and knees and began to climb down. Sarah stood in the closet and lit up the hole with the flashlight.

"Do you see anything?" Sarah asked

For a short time Melody didn't answer. Sarah shined the flashlight toward what seemed to be the bottom, but could barely see her anymore. It seemed to be at least ten feet down to the bottom and pitch black. Not even the beam from the flashlight completely penetrated the darkness.

"No, but I made it to the bottom" Melody finally answered back, "get ready, it is really cold and damp down here, wherever 'here' is…"

Melody untied the rope from her waist and told Sarah pulled up the rope and come down. Sarah pulled the rope to the top, tied it to her waist and started down into the hole. Loosing grip on the flashlight, it fell to the bottom into a pile of burlap bags. Melody picked up the undamaged flashlight and shined it toward Sarah as she climbed down to the bottom.

Sarah and Melody stood still and followed the light beam from the flashlight, looking around the room. From where the bedroom was above them they should be standing in the kitchen or the living room, but this was definitely some place else! Maybe Ashley was right about everything, and this was where the devils came from. The girls continued to search.

The room looked more like the inside of a barn. There was an old lawn mower, some rakes and shovels, and large pieces of equipment that a farmer would use in the fields to cut straw for farm animals. The air was cold and musty. The girls could feel the goose bumps growing on their arms. Suddenly, the beam of light caught a moving shadow. It moved along the wall just a few feet away.

Melody shined the flashlight in the direction of the shadow. It was that black shadow figure they had seen in the wine cellar. It stopped a few feet away and seemed to be watching them, not moving. The room had a dead silence. Then without warning, it swiftly shot off and disappeared into the wall! Melody and Sarah took one step back, their hands on their mouths, trying not to panic. The shadow figure seemed to be following them throughout the house. But why, what did it want from them?

"There has to be another way out of here," Sarah said. Melody guided the beam of light once more around the room. At the opposite end of the room from where they were standing, were two tall wood doors. They were latched in the middle with a large piece of wood. Melody and Sarah started yelling out to Belinda, but heard nothing. They continued to search through the barn, but found no one else there.

"Wait Mel, move the beam of light back…right there," said Sarah as she took a hold of Melody's wrist and guided her in the direction she was talking about. "What is it?" Melody said. "I know I saw something, THERE IN THE CORNER!" Sarah replied frantically. They could see two sets of glowing dots off in the darkness that looked like eyes. As the girls watched, the red glowing eyes began to move in their direction.

They needed to get on the other side of the tall wood doors. Sarah and Melody hurried over to the doors and together they lifted the heavy piece of wood. With one big push, they swung the wood lock out of the way. The doors creaked loudly as they opened slowly outward. Melody peeked her head out of the barn and quickly looked around. They were back by the woods behind the house, or at least it looked that way! Maybe this was a completely different

place! At least they were out where it was well lit and away

from whatever it was back in the barn.

CHAPTER FIFTEEN

As they hurried from the barn there was a small path that led off into the woods. Melody and Sarah kept looking back at the barn to make sure that no one was following them. As they turned a small curve in the path, they could see someone. Up ahead they could see what looked like Belinda. The black shadow figure and a woman in a long old-fashioned blue gown were following her. Melody and Sarah started to run, trying to catch up with her, yelling out her name as they ran. Belinda seemed to ignore them. They finally caught up with Belinda and Sarah grabbed her by the arm to stop her and turn her around.

The shadow figure and the woman stopped and turned to look at them. The woman looked like the picture in the locked they had found in the diary. She looked angrily at Sarah and Melody. The black shadows face was still hidden from view by the hood he had over his head. It seemed as though the black shadow and the woman were trying to protect Belinda.

"Belinda, why didn't you answer us?" Sarah asked, holding on firmly the Belinda's arm.

Still Belinda said nothing looking blankly at Sarah. She seemed to be in the same kind of trance as Ashley was under. Her arms were limp and she seemed fragile and weak. Her face was a white as freshly fallen snow, and she had large blackened sags under her eyes. The girls tried shaking her and talking in her ear. Nothing seemed to bring Belinda back into reality.

"Answer us Belinda, what's wrong… what's going on?" Melody said firmly, feeling as though Belinda was playing some kind of awful game.

"I am not Belinda, my name is Ashley!" Belinda finally acknowledged, pulling her arm from Sarah's grip. Sarah grabbed Belinda's arm once again. "I have to go, I have to help my sister!" she said as tears fell from her eyes.

"You are Belinda," Melody said sharply, "Your not Ashley!"

Belinda pulled her arm back and broke free from Sarah. She started running down the path. The black shadow figure and the woman followed close behind her. Their feet were not touching the ground. The black shadow and the woman just glided through the air.

Melody and Sarah ran as fast as they could. They tried to keep up with Belinda, but they were falling further and further behind. They tripped over sticks and brambles that were scattered across the path. Soon they came upon the field next to the lake. Now they knew that they had been here before. How could the trap door in Ashley's closet lead here, this was so confusing. Sarah and Melody stopped where the path ended and watched to see what was going to happen next. They watched Belinda and the two other beings moving along the lakes edge.

Belinda and the two figures continued to the area of the lake side where Laura had gone in to save Jimmy and disappeared. It was hard to see, so Melody and Sarah ran up to the lakes edge. They stopped about ten yards from Belinda and tried to catch their breath. As the girls walked closer they could see Belinda point, showing the black shadow and the woman where Laura and Jimmy had drowned. She began crying violently.

"I was walking along the far side of the lake from here when I saw Laura and Jimmy in trouble. I ran over to the other side of the lake as fast as I could, trying to get closer to them. I tried to save them, I really did. There was nothing I could do! Laura went under before I could grab her!" Belinda told the shadow figure and the woman. "I thought that you would hate me forever for letting them die," Belinda continued.

Belinda knelt down in the soft dirt next to the lake and sobbed. The shadow figure and the woman swooped over and seemed to envelop Belinda in a hug. They talked to Belinda for a moment, telling her that they understood and that it wasn't her fault that Laura and Jimmy had drown. Then they slowly moved out over the water and disappeared. Belinda lifted her head and looked at Melody and Sarah, tears still filling her eyes and falling down her cheeks.

"Where am I?" Belinda said, looking lost and bewildered.

Belinda looked up at Sarah and Melody. "You mean you don't know what happened?" Melody asked as she pulled a tissue from her book bag.

"No, the last thing I remember was looking out of the attic window over-looking the driveway at the house," Belinda said, truly not sure what had happened to her. Mel and Sarah explained to Belinda everything that happened since the girls were in the attic. They told her about the trap door in the floor of the closet and the fact that her body had been taken over by Ashley. Belinda, listening to all of this, felt confused and disoriented.

Things were finally starting to make sense to Melody, and she started pulling it all together. First, the black shadow figure was the father, Mr. Marshall, who had been watching the girls every move since they had entered the Elmwood Mansion. Then, the locket with the pictures inside was Laura and her mother, just as they had thought in the beginning. She was also the woman who was walking with the black shadow figure and Belinda on the path through the woods. The little boy, with the playful sense of humor they saw slamming the door, was Laura and Ashley's younger brother. But the trance that Belinda seemed to be under was difficult to understand, and how Ashley took over her body.

Then Melody remembered that they read about one of the children having mental problems. Ashley seemed to be in a dream state when they had first entered her bedroom when they heard her screaming. Ashley had tried the doorknob to the closet and could not get it open, but Melody was able to. Maybe Ashley was sleep-walking, or maybe, because of her fragility, she was the one with mental problems. Because of Ashley's fear of the devils she saw, could have been the guilt she felt because she was unable to save Laura and Jimmy. She seemed to know that she was a ghost and could no longer do it on her own. She used Belinda's body to go into the closet and in through the trap door, because she was too afraid to go on her own. That must have been why the shadow figure and the woman treated Belinda like she was their daughter.

Also, in the woods Belinda said that she was Ashley. Now it was clear that Ashley was replaying the acts of that terrible day through Belinda. She wanted her parents to know that she was at the lake that day. Jimmy and Laura had drowned and she tried to save them, but didn't get there in time. Because Ashley loved her brother and sister so much, it haunted her even after death. Prior to Ashley's death, the whole ordeal had become too much for her and eventually drove her crazy. This is what had caused her horrifying nightmares that made everyone conclude that she had psychological problems. Because of all of the turmoil that the Marshall family had encountered, maybe that was the reason for the so-called haunting. No one could rest in peace until they had all of the answers they needed.

Sarah and Melody stood up and helped Belinda to her feet. Belinda, still lost in thought, followed her sister and Sarah back through the woods and down the path. Belinda looked back one last time at the lake. At the end of the path, Melody and Sarah half expected to see the house, but instead they were back at the old barn.

The doors were swinging wildly in the breeze. They were thinking about the red glowing eyes they had seen as they were leaving the barn earlier. Neither Sarah nor Melody mentioned the red glowing eyes they saw to Belinda. The girls hurried and made their way into the barn and found the tree that led back to Ashley's bedroom. They began climbing the steps of the tree, sending Belinda up first.

Melody was last to go up the steps. She glanced one last time around the barn. Suddenly, Melody could see the red glowing eyes moving quickly toward her. As she started to climb the steps her foot slipped and she fell to the floor. Melody looked up and saw the glowing eyes getting closer. She hurried back to her feet and grabbed one of the steps above her head and rushed up the steps as fast as she could.

When Melody finally made it back into the closet, Sarah took her hand and helped her to her feet. "My, you look like you saw a ghost!" Sarah said with a chuckle. Melody's face was pale and she looked shaken. "Hurry, close the trap door!" Melody said. Sarah grabbed the door and slammed it shut. "Those glowing eyes we saw in the barn earlier were chasing after me as I was climbing up the steps!" Melody said.

As they walked out of the closet into the bedroom they saw Belinda and Ashley standing in the middle of the room.

"Thank you for helping me," Ashley said, "Maybe now my nightmares will finally come to an end. She looked at the girls with a small smile and then slowly vanished.

CHAPTER SIXTEEN

The house didn't seem so spooky anymore, just sad. They seemed like a normal family that had endured some horrible problems. Most of the information the girls compiled from the library had to do with things that happened after the house was abandoned back in 1938. Only a few details were mentioned about the Marshall family. Details like the drowning that took place and Ashley's mental problems.

The girls sat down on the side of Ashley's bed and

147

continued to read Laura's diary. They felt good about being able to help Ashley through her dilemma. Maybe now she could rest peacefully. Ashley's mental problems stemmed from the nightmares that haunted her over and over again. She could not come to terms with the fact that she couldn't save Jimmy and Laura at the lake.

After reading the diary further, the girls found more interesting information. Doctor's tried a type of hypnosis, but nothing seemed to work for her. The devils that Ashley saw were how she portrayed her parents. She worried about how her parents would react if they knew about Laura and Jimmy. She thought that her parents would hate her forever because she didn't save them and she always thought that she could have done something more.

The devils, which were her fears, haunted her every day. Ashley never mentioned the devils she saw to anyone except for Melody and Sarah. She feared that people would think that she had gone completely over the edge.

The diamonds found in the wood box with the diary

belonged to Laura's mother. Laura had found the diamonds in one of the drawers of her father's desk. She didn't know how valuable they were or that they were diamonds, and put them in the box for safekeeping. Laura was saving them to give to her mother for Christmas. Laura loved her mother very much and kept her locket with the picture of her mother with her in her secret place by the lake. Laura and Jimmy thought they were the only one's that knew about the diary and the secret hiding place. They didn't know that Ashley always spied on them when they went to the lake.

The little boy was Johnny, who Laura found to be a clown. He would constantly play tricks on her, just trying to make her laugh. He was always getting into trouble, but Laura loved Johnny very much and was very protective of the little boy.

Now that the girls seemed to know the family better, it seemed odd that there was no information about what had happened to them in the end. Did they miss something at the library? Why did they abandon the house in 1938...what happened? They could not have all just vanished! This is the part that didn't make any sense, and the girls were determined to find out. They knew too much to just leave it all like this, they needed to know the whole truth. The story about the Marshall family seemed to be coming to a close, and the girls were exhausted.

Sarah, Melody, and Belinda knew that their parents would be getting really worried about them. They closed up the diary and put in back in Sarah's book bag. It would take over an hour to walk back to their bikes and ride home, which by that point it would be getting dark. The girls followed one another out of the bedroom and down the hall to the staircase that led back to the foyer.

Suddenly, the black shadow came out of nowhere and was standing at the foot of the steps looking up at the girls! He removed his black hood and revealed what he truly looked like. He looked just like the painting in the room with the desk. They knew it was Mr. Marshall since the moment when they saw him walking with Mrs. Marshall and Belinda.

"The diamonds," Mr. Marshall said firmly, "I want the diamonds back! He stood stout with his feet closely together, his eyes beaming at them.

The girls just stood there, frozen in place at the top of the steps. Then Sarah grabbed her book bag from her back and began fumbling through it. She could feel the wood box in her hands and pulled it out.

"Give me the diamonds NOW!" Mr. Marshall said, angrily.

Sarah opened the box and picked out the diamonds one, two, three, four, five, six. They were all there. Then Sarah laid her book bag on the step and moved slowly toward Mr. Marshall. Melody and Belinda stayed close behind her. When she got close enough, she held out her hand with the diamonds.

"We didn't mean to steal the diamonds," Sarah said hesitantly, "we found them in a wooden box Laura and Jimmy had hidden by the lake."

With that she dropped the diamonds into Mr.

Marshall's out stretched hand. He slowly brought his head down looking at the diamonds and nodded, as if saying thank you. Without another word, he disappeared.

"Why did I know he would do that?" Melody said chuckling, trying to hide the fact that she felt shaky inside. "They always vanish as quickly as they appear around here."

The girls continued down the last couple of steps into the foyer. Though they had a fun adventure, they were glad that it was over. They were all very tired and hungry, and they really needed to get going. Melody went to the front door and tried to open it, but it was locked. She tried over and over again, but the door would not budge. "WE ARE TRAPPED IN HERE!" Melody yelled out.

CHAPTER SEVENTEEN

Melody tried the front door one last time, frantically jiggling the lock back and forth, but it would not open. Belinda and Sarah tried the door as well with no luck. "This can't be happening to us!" Belinda said, her face going pale, "MAYBE WE ARE TRAPPED!"

Sarah ran over to one of the windows in the living room and tried to open it. Nothing, it was jammed and now the girls new that they were trapped. The girls began looking

153

for something to break one of the windows when a fireball erupted in the fireplace. The flames blew out of the fireplace wall by about four feet and caught the curtains on fire. Quickly the room began to fill with smoke! Belinda grabbed a chair from the corner of the room and ran over to the window. She hit the window as hard as she could, but the glass wouldn't break.

Melody grabbed the sheet that was still partially covering the sofa and ran over to try to smother the fire, but it was too late. The flames had already engulfed the one wall and were traveling across the ceiling. The smoke was so thick that the girls coughed, trying the get some air, and dropping to their knees. Crawling on their knees they finally made it back into the foyer. Sarah, almost completely breathless, held on to the banister at the foot of the staircase.

"The kitchen door!" Sarah said, barely getting the words out of her mouth. The girls felt their way down the hall next to the staircase and into the kitchen. By now the smoke was so thick it was hard to see anything. They finally made it across the kitchen floor to the doors that led into the courtyard. They were locked as well. Sarah remembered the pocket knife that was in her book bag. She pulled the book bag from her back, unzipped it, and began fumbling around. Melody and Belinda were barely able to see, watching Sarah. Finding the knife, she opened it and started to pry on the lock, but it was no use.

"Maybe we can use that knife on the front door," Melody said holding her hands up to her face. Belinda and Sarah both agreed and they quickly headed for the front door. Making it back to the front foyer, the girls heard a loud crashing noise above them.

At about that very moment, Johnny came stumbling down the staircase, heading for the front door. As he reached the door he fell to the floor, his little hand reaching for the knob. For that brief moment he seemed whole and real. He reached up a second time, but was unable to reach. His hand fell to the floor and he closed his eyes. Screams came from the upstairs as the girls watched what was left of the living room go up in flames.

Suddenly, from nowhere, Mrs. Marshall appeared. She bent down and picked up Johnny and looked at the girls on the floor of the foyer. Then Mrs. Marshall and Johnny disappeared as they drifted back up the steps. The front doors blew open, almost pulling them off their hinges. Sarah, Belinda, and Melody struggled and crawled along the foyer floor out on to the front porch of the house. The girls, coughing and gasping for air, finally made it to their feet and moved away from the house into the driveway. As they stood up turned around they could hear windows breaking and glass was raining down around them. The flames were now engulfing the entire house. They could still hear the screams coming from the upstairs windows.

"The house was never abandoned," Melody said still coughing, "they were trapped in the fire and died here!"

Off in the distance, the girls could hear sirens. Sounds of the fire trucks and rescue units faded out the screams from the Marshall's until they were nonexistent. The girls hugged each other in one long embrace, grateful to have escaped the burning house. They thought about the Marshall family and that the information seemed entirely wrong. Now, the girls knew the entire truth, except for the fact that the information that they found at the library said that the house was abandoned, it never mentioned the fire.

It was now getting quite dark, and they could see the headlights on the dirt road coming closer, the sirens getting louder and louder until they were deafening. Two fire trucks and an ambulance stopped in front of the house. Firemen were running around wildly grabbing hoses to put out the fire.

Two paramedics ran over to the girls who were now sitting against a tree in front of the house. As they started to check the girls, Melody could see her and Sarah's parents searching around. One of the paramedics yelled over to them as they came closer, "there over here and seem to be just fine!"

Their parents had found out only a few hours prior to all of this that the girls were not where they said they would be. They called around to all of the neighbors and then went to the police station to place a missing persons report. While at the police station a report of a fire came in, informing the officers that "Squad Three", was on its way to the old Marshall mansion. Right away, the Drakes remembered seeing some information on Melody's dresser the week before and informed the officers. They called Sarah's parents who met them at the mansion.

Melody, Belinda, and Sarah knew they were in the biggest trouble ever as their parents came over to embrace them, thankful that they were all right. "What is the matter with you girls?" Mrs. Drake said sobbing. The girls apologized to their parents for lying to them and promised they would never pull anything like that again. They followed the paramedics back where the ambulance was waiting to take them to the hospital for a thorough check up. The girls knew they had learned a big lesson that night as they thought of Mrs. Marshall and how she had seemingly saved their lives.

Later that evening, around 9:30, the girls arrived home from the hospital. Their parents tucked them into bed and told them to get a good night sleep. In the morning the girls would have a lot of explaining to do. Melody wondered how Sarah was doing and what kind of trouble she would have to face.

She watched her parents leave the room and then snuggled her head into her pillow. She couldn't stop thinking about the Marshall family. They had almost become a part of her and she felt sorry for them. Feeling warm and safe in their own beds, the girls fell sound asleep.

CHAPTER EIGHTEEN

The next morning during breakfast the girls explained

to their parents about why they did what they had done and all

the experiences they had met. Their parents seemed like they

didn't believe what the girls had seen and that they talked to

the ghosts of the Marshall family, but they were willing to try.

It still didn't excuse the fact that they had lied and that what

they had done was very dangerous. Their parents agreed to

let them off easy since they went through such an

extraordinary ordeal. They felt that the girls had been through enough and had taught themselves a good lesson.

Later that day Melody remembered the poetry assignment she had to finish. She decided to spend the rest of her day writing down some of the experiences she had at the Marshall mansion to complete the assignment. She felt that the real truth had to be known about the Marshall family. Or in reality, the Marshall family would finally be able to tell their own story. Melody knew that most people would not believe what the girls had seen at the mansion.

It was the middle of the afternoon when Melody finally finished her poetry assignment. She had not talked to Sarah since the night before and decided to call her. She picked up her school work from the bed where she had been working and neatly placed them in her book bag. She went back and sat on the bed side and picked up the phone from the night table. Melody dialed Sarah's number and waited. The phone seemed to be ringing of the hook. Melody walked over to her bedroom window and looked over at Sarah's house.

All of the cars were in the driveway and the front door was open. Curious, Melody walked back over by the bed and hung up the phone.

Melody went downstairs and informed her mom that she was going to check on Sarah. As she crossed the street and started walking up Sarah's driveway, she could hear voices coming from the back yard. Belinda and Sarah were sitting on the back porch and Sarah's parents were out cleaning up the yard.

"Hey you guys!" Melody said as she pulled a chair up next to Belinda and sat down. "I wondered where you were, I tried to call a little while ago and there was no answer."

The girls sat for a while and talked. They were still very overwhelmed by what had happened to them. Sarah had explained everything to her parents, and they were stunned and didn't seem to believe her. They tried to be understanding just as Melody's parents had been.

Still curious about the house, and feeling bad about the Marshall family, the girls decided to take one last ride to the house. Melody and Belinda went home and asked for permission to go after Sarah's parents had said it was okay. Soon they were on their bikes, heading for the mansion. They had to be back before dinner, so they didn't have too much time. This time they rode their bikes all the way up to where the house used to stand.

The mansion was now just a pile of burned rubble and ashes. The girls laid their bikes down and stood staring at the pile in front of them. "Did you hear that," Sarah said in almost a whisper.

"What," Melody asked. The three stood there for a moment and listened.

"That, I hear it now too," Belinda said, "it's voices, I hear voices."

Somehow, in the pile of ashes and debris, a jumbling of voices could be heard. The girls could not understand what the voices were saying. It sounded like a small crowd of people all talking at the same time in a low whisper. The Marshall's were still here!

Rumors had gone around about the mansion coming back to life on its own. One thing that was said in the Sunday morning paper was that the house had burned to the ground years ago. People had come back later to find the house unscathed and just as beautiful as ever. Maybe those things did happen, but this time the house still lay in a pile of debris. Maybe the Marshall's and the stories about their family were now ready to be put to rest.

Knowing that their parents would want them back home soon for dinner, the girls picked up their bikes and started on their way home. As they rode home, they all agreed on an idea to write their own article about the house for the Danville Gazette. Just as their parents had found their story to be unbelievable, maybe the people in Danville would as well. It didn't matter though; it was the truth that would make the difference.

AUTHOR'S NOTES

As a young girl of about nine years of age, I can recall having one of the most terrifying dreams. It was a dream that seemed to reach inside me and grab on to my soul. It was like a dream with bright vivid pictures that I will remember for the rest of my life.

I can remember waking up and walking to the foot of the bed. There on the floor, was a small throw rug that I pulled away revealing a trap door. There was a leather strap on the door that I grabbed on to and swung the door open.

Looking down into the hole in the floor, I could not see anything. Suddenly, with only a thought, a flashlight appeared in my hand. I turned it on and again looked into the hole. Small strips of wood were nailed to a tree that rose to the opening in the floor. I climbed down the steps into a large garage. Tools and large equipment was scattered all about the garage. I stumbled through the garage to a small door on the far side and opened it.

Outside I could see a path that led off into the woods. I followed the long narrow path to a clearing where an old house was standing. Curious, I walked up and opened the large doors in the front of the house. Once inside the old house, I saw the black shadow figure standing at the top of a large set of curved steps. It began to move toward me. I could feel my heart pounding rapidly. Terrified, I ran from the house and back down the path to the garage and went inside to hide.

As I sat crouched in the corner, I could see red glowing devils moving toward me. They started to chase me; their eye's glowing brightly as they waved their pitchforks. Seeing them, I knew I had to get away.

I somehow found my way passed the devilish creatures. I began to climb the steps of the tree as quickly as I could, my heart pounding so fast, giving me a choking feeling in my throat. Finally reaching the top, I climbed back into my bedroom and slammed the trap door shut and hurried to my feet.

Snakes were everywhere, crawling through my toes. I ran across the room to escape them! Finding myself in front of the closet I began working the switches on the wall trying desperately to turn on the lights! Nothing happened. I had the attic bedroom that extended the full length of the house. I decided to walk over and sit at the top of the steps.

My father, who was awake downstairs heard my cries and came up to put me back to bed. He walked over to the light switches on the wall and proved to me that the lights were working okay before he went back downstairs. He also assured me that there weren't any snakes in the room so I could get back to sleep.

I remember that it was storming outside all that night. I must have been sleep-walking and because of the storm, the lights had temporarily gone out. By the time my father had come upstairs, the electricity had come back on and he was able to set my mind at ease.

I had a lot of wild dreams as I was growing up, as do most young children, but this is the one that I remember the most. I wrote about the dream in a diary that I kept long ago. Where that diary is now, I am not quite sure. Over the years I improvised on the dream. If I close my eyes I can recall the dream and all of the terrifying feelings that came with it.